TO SPEAK OF THINGS UNSEEN

HEMSTREET WITCHES BOOK 2

RAIN TRUEAX

To Speak of Things Unseen

By

Rain Trueax

Nothing is ever
What it appears to be

To Speak of Things Unseen

Hemstreet Witches Book 2

is an original work of Rain Trueax.

All rights reserved.

Copyright © 2016   Rain Trueax

ISBN: 978-1-943537-11-2
Paperback

Prepared and presented by:

Seven Oaks
Monmouth, Or.

Sign up for new release notifications at http://raintrueax.blogspot.com

Personal Contact and Rights Agreements write to: raintrueax@gmail.com

CHAPTER 1

Mellow Yellow Boutique—Tucson, Arizona
July 19, 2014, Friday

"Ms. Hemstreet?" the young woman's voice quavered with uncertainty as she came from the summer heat into the cooler air of the shop.

"Yes, may I help you?" Elke asked. The girl was wearing flip-flops, shorts and a t-shirt that said *normal people are so weird*. Nothing looked new. Hardly likely, she could afford any of the clothing in the shop as she glanced at the racks of designer knock-offs. When her gaze met Elke's, she blinked several times.

"Does the incense bother you?" Elke asked.

"The girl shook her head. "I just..."

Elke waited. She wasn't surprised the girl had realized she was in the wrong shop.

"I've been told... that is... I heard you are a witch." Her voice grew a bit stronger.

Elke let out a breath. "Goodness, wherever did you hear such a thing?"

"It was a friend of Mr. Braddock. Do you know Mr. Braddock?"

"Distantly." She narrowed her eyes as she studied the young woman. How much did she really know about the punishment dealt out to that perverse wizard?

"Well. He used to... That is he sometimes did favors for people and could make others do what they might not want to do."

"Then go visit him. I am not someone who wants to make anyone do what they don't wish." Elke noticed the storm clouds were darkening the sky. Had this girl come accompanied by a spirit? She looked toward the door, sensing nothing to tell her. The shop was protected by wards, but they'd been broken through before. Tucson sheltered spirits and humans of all types—the seen and the unseen. Burglar alarms didn't work for everything.

"I was told that Mr. Braddock had a stroke. He can't... that is he's not... I am desperate Ms. Hemstreet. I truly need help right now. I need a spell."

"Who told you such a thing about Mr. Braddock or me?"

The girl's demeanor changed from placating to sly. It would not be the first time the local newspaper had sent someone to try to get a story. Since the murders of the late spring, there'd been nothing much to sell papers. With the heat reaching epic proportions, the city felt drained. Those who remained, who couldn't escape to the north were quiet, hiding from the heat, and often in rotten moods.

"I could pay you, if you are worried I'd be asking a favor," the girl said. Now Elke felt sure that she was not who she was pretending to be. The question though was-- what was she?

"Everyone knows witches don't exist," she said as a test.

"They do exist, and they can even do curses if someone can pay them." The girl's voice turned more strident. Amazing how quickly someone could go from being a supplicant to an attacker. Not the first time Elke had seen that.

"You have been misinformed. And you are looking for the wrong thing if you seek a spell or potion to manipulate another."

"You don't understand." Tears ran down her cheeks.

She was good. Elke would give her that. She should be in the little theater. "Even if such a thing were possible, not saying I believe it is, it would come back to hurt you."

"I am hurting now."

Determined. "Looking for magick answers to earthly problems avoids what led to them in the first place." Torre would have been better at handling this. Elke knew herself too well. She quickly grew impatient with those looking for a shortcut in life.

"You don't understand."

Elke resisted the loud sigh. Would the story she was about to hear be true or created to deceive? She was sorely tempted to use her psychic powers, but it would be for a selfish purpose, using magick to solve a problem, which she had just told the girl was a mistake.

"Where did you hear that I was a witch," she asked as she handed the young woman a cup of water.

"It's out there on the street."

"Where is there?"

The girl watched her and then the tears started again. "Alan said he loved me and then… now he's marrying Michelle." There was a loud sob. "I know he doesn't love her. He loves me. I need something to make him know it too."

"What is your name?"

"Jessica. I think Michelle put him under a spell. I need a more powerful witch, and I heard your family is powerful."

By now, she knew it would do no good, but she tried again. "Heard from whom?"

"Just… the er street talk."

"Well, you heard wrong. I sell clothing."

The girl looked up, wiping away tears. "Could you make a potion to help me not care? I'd pay you."

Elke shook her head. "Affairs of the heart have nothing to do with witchcraft." Why was saying something once never enough? "Even if I was what you thought, it'd be a terrible injustice to interfere."

"I went to El Tiradito, the wishing shrine. I put my candle there like it said to do and made a wish. I went back in the morning and it was still burning. Doesn't that mean I get my wish?"

Elke worked to restrain her instinctive, snarky retort. "Then you have no problem."

"You really won't help me." The young woman's voice turned strident and angry.

"It would not be a help—even if I was what you'd been told."

Jessica handed back the drained paper cup. "You just don't want to help," she snapped as she hurried out the door Denali had just opened.

"What was that about?" Elke's older sister asked watching the young woman stalk away.

"I am not sure. Maybe a reporter. Maybe love gone awry. Maybe a spy." She gave a little laugh.

"My, you are suspicious."

"It's a personality trait. So what can I do for the new bride?" She tried not to put a caustic twist to it. She wasn't really jealous, but Denali getting married had taken her best friend away from her.

"Actually I need a dress and something to travel in. Nick has two openings, which apparently I must dutifully attend as his wife—and to keep all the little fans from trying to steal him away."

Elke chuckled. "Fat chance of that. He's totally enamored —for now."

"Don't give me a bad time."

"Of course not. Well..." She rubbed her hands together with pretend glee. "How much can we set you back for?"

"I thought as a sister, I'd get a discount."

"What?" she asked with mock shock. "You need to take advantage of your poor sisters' shop when you are married to a wildly successful painter?"

"It was worth a try."

An hour later, with two dresses on hangers and protected by plastic, from what looked to be a promised afternoon thunderstorm, Denali was out the door, and Elke went back to tagging new merchandise.

She thought about her visitor who had very quickly turned from supplicant to antagonist. Instincts told her the girl had no boyfriend and either worked for someone trying to prove the Hemstreets were witches, or was a reporter hoping for a story. She regretted not getting her last name. Of course, it likely would have been a lie.

Although Tucson had been a tolerant city, where it came to spirits and spirit workers, a new zeitgeist seemed to be growing—one that operated on fear. It had grown with the help of two, seemingly unsolved murders—murders with a touch of the macabre to make them even more horrifying. Fear of the unknown was one of the most powerful forces to manipulate people and force through agendas that went against their own best interests. Fear overrode commonsense.

She wished more people grasped the true nature of the spirit world and the consequences of tampering with it. Natural witches, such as her family, understood the responsibility, to which they had been born. Their goal was always to make the world a better place. Their purpose was to neutralize or eliminate those who would misuse earth and spirit powers. More humans needed to understand there were good entities out there but also those who would destroy if given a chance.

She had just finished reading a book filled with adventure, monsters, abusive humans, demons, and a hero who fought with the same values she'd been taught. In between the action, the writer had scenes that argued for the obligation to use spiritual powers when the cause was just. *Vislogus* was fiction, of course, but the powers were anything but. She would have to talk to her mother about it and see if she had read it. It had gone up the bestseller lists, but when she had looked, there appeared to be nothing about its author—beyond his name.

Barrio Viejo – Tucson, Arizona

In her upstairs apartment, Elke changed into shorts and a t-shirt, turned up the air conditioning, poured herself a chilled chardonnay, and opened a box of leftovers from the last meal she'd had at *Mi Nidito*. She tried to remember how old they were, but they smelled safe. After two hours at the gym, to burn off her frustration, she was too tired to cook or care and set them in the microwave.

Her love of Mexican food had led her to experiment with pretty much every such restaurant in Tucson. The *nopalito* enchilada at this one had proven her favorite. The date that night had not been. The fact that Asa Taggert had as little interest in her as she had in him hadn't been a surprise. It had been a surprise when, after an event to discuss development in the barrio, he had asked her to dinner. Perhaps, his hope had been she might support his political career. Lots of luck with that. He might be a rising star in his party, which was not hers, but his stand on growth was more oriented toward making money than preserving history and culture. She wanted to see the barrios maintain their dignity and identity. He seemed more interested in development and dollars.

No one would deny Asa was exceedingly handsome, dark, saturnine, well dressed, lean, and surprisingly muscular. He hadn't gotten that body eating at fundraisers. If she hadn't realized how important politics could be to a community, and felt a responsibility because of her family's investments in Tucson's businesses, she'd have never attended another. Unfortunately, that wasn't an option.

As she ate, she watched as a bicyclist pedaled down the street. She could almost see the sweat dripping off him. Crazy to be out in this heat, even at dusk—and risky given the drunk drivers. She saved her exercising for the gym where she could work out in air-conditioned comfort—with any sweat coming from her exertion.

She had purchased her condo on the second floor of what had at one time been one of the barrio's fine mansions. It now provided three homes. She had the entire second floor to herself. Beyond the street, she could see 'A' Mountain. To the south, black storm clouds were piling up. Maybe there was hope for a wet storm. The first storms of the monsoon season had blown past, and Tucson was waiting for the next. Only storms would cool the night-- short of the arrival of October.

After polishing off the leftovers, she refilled her wine glass and went out onto the deck that overlooked the enclosed lush backyard. It benefited from the main floor residence of Maya Rudolph, a woman of uncertain years, who loved flowers. She knew the right ones to draw birds and butterflies. The garden was alive with activity. Even in the wicked heat of summer, Maya found a way to keep her flowers blooming and not withering. This was a delightful advantage for Elke, who admired gardening but had no sense of how to do it. All it required from her was a wave and smile when Maya was in her garden. Since evenings were generally when Maya watched her favorite television programs, the garden was generally exclusively Elke's to enjoy, to watch the sky turn crimson beyond the Tucson Mountains, to feel the air shift and gentle breezes cool the night.

In the distance, she heard mourning doves cooing. A street over, someone practiced a piano. The pianist was having a hard time, stopping, missing a note, starting again. She could imagine groans to go along with it.

In the smaller condo below, fragrances of something delicious wafted up. Tony Tremaine had suggested she come for dinner a time or two, but she wasn't interested in dating a neighbor where it wouldn't work out and then how embarrassing. Better to stay distant acquaintances.

She settled into the soft lawn chair, after checking to be sure that no scorpions had taken up residence. She thought again about *Vislogus*.

How could the author know so much about magick and its potential for good or evil? She'd read many books where the authors had no clue about the reality of the world she knew. Mitchell Ford did.

All her attempts to learn more about the reclusive author had hit dead ends. Didn't authors want publicity, go on book tours, try to be on television shows, but he'd done none of that. His book had caught some kind of sci-fi/fantasy zeitgeist and soared high, without the author appearing to have lifted a finger. That made him mysterious and a source of speculation. Beyond knowing he lived in Arizona, her research had turned up nothing. Two online tabloid photographs had been at such a distance it left him unrecognizable. He was hiding away from the prominence that naturally went with such a popular novel. The question was why?

She had even gone so far as to break one of her personal taboos. Holding his book, she had closed her eyes and tried fruitlessly to conjure up the creator's image. It had been for purely selfish reasons. She had tried to convince herself that her motives had been pure—needing to understand the source of the wisdom in the book. She had fooled no one, least of all herself.

Tapping in her mother's number, she heard the phone ringing, almost closed it.

"What do you want, dear?" her mother asked in that deep, almost sexy voice even when talking to her daughters.

"Are you familiar with *Vislogus*?"

"Isn't everyone?" Her mother chuckled.

"What do you know about its author?"

"Why?"

"I am impressed with the book, have been considering whether it could work into a play for our little theater." She hadn't even said that in her mind, but she knew it had been back there.

"I'd say that was quite a longshot."

"Why?"

"Mitchell Ford has not let anyone use it. I have been told that a major studio offered an unheard of sum for the rights, and he just laughed at them."

"Do you know him?"

"I have seen him at a meeting once, but no introduction and did not talk to him."

"What does he look like?"

Her mother laughed. "It was awhile back. I can just say he's extraordinarily tall."

She had a feeling her mother knew more than she revealed. "I'd like to arrange to meet him."

There was a silence. "You would? For what purpose?" She recognized that tone. Her mother was projecting, way beyond what she was asking. That could only mean matchmaking. With one daughter married, her mother was plotting overtime to see the rest with a mate-- next would be wanting grandchildren.

"I told you the purpose," she said restraining her annoyance. After all, it was logical a mother would want her daughters happily married and at twenty-seven, some were married with babies-- nothing that was on Elke's own agenda—especially not the baby part.

"As it happens, I do know someone who knows him well enough —if he wants to get involved. I'll see what I can do and get back to you." She could hear the smile in her mother's voice, as she hung up. Fine, let her imagine all she wanted. Elke's purposes had nothing to do with a romantic interest—or so she told herself.

When it cooled off enough for sleeping, she stripped, shoved the sheets down, and contemplated how easy it would be to fall asleep. She tried to push the book from her thoughts but it was there, the scenes, especially the hero, Adolfo Lupan.

As a wizard, he had been called to a mysterious place, undefined in the book, but there were dangers there, beings such as she'd never seen, perhaps no one had. He had fought a deadly battle, nearly been killed, but he had succeeded in bringing order to the region by killing and forcing to leave whoever the enemy had been. As Ford had with the setting for the book, he'd kept the details of the beings vague. Aliens maybe? She wasn't sure. *Vislogus* ,also, never described what Adolfo looked like. That part wasn't important. It was what he could do, like shapeshifting, and that was very in tune with what Elke knew was possible—that and much more.

Adolfo paid a high price for his heroism. Each time he used his powers, he drained his strength, which required a time to build back up—if he had that time. Despite his magick powers, he put his life at risk. He was the warrior and sacrificial hero all in one. Powerful obviously, but also noble in his desire to make the world a better place, at any personal cost.

As a witch, Elke understood some of the feeling of being drained--

but more had been described as taken from Adolfo than she'd experienced. But she'd also never gone into a real war as he had. What would it be like to face, not just human evil, but something that was supposed to be mythological? She remembered the books she'd read about Native American gods and monsters. She needed to get them out again. Might they be as real as Adolfo's powers?

She'd been taught to fight using earth elementals. She knew how to shoot plasma bolts, control their power, use swords, bullets, and knives infused with platinum-osmirdium alloy. She could transport herself from one place to another, go invisible when required, and look into people's minds. One of her greatest joys was shifting into a wolf and roaming the desert as an animal.

What she had never done is what had most fascinated her about the fictional Adolfo-- he hunted monsters. He found them in their lairs, on the earth or in the sky. He had used weapons she understood but added an element she had not known. If these monsters had in anyway threatened or used their power, it had left a scent he could track, and when he found them, he showed no mercy.

Ford's book claimed it was fiction, but something about it seemed real. Was that why she could not release it or him? If her mother could not find a source to let her meet Mitchell Ford, she would find him another way.

She sent her intentions into the universe. As a last resort, she would use her powers, no matter how much she'd been told to never do that for selfish reasons. When she found the writer, he would lead her to Lupan. Ford had to know him. While the plot may have been a device, fictional-- too many elements were real. Lupan was real. She felt his energy. He was not imaginary. She would find him.

∽

Tucson, Arizona

Watching the human drama play out below, Ornis felt his usual satisfaction—a demonic job well done on both sides of the havoc he was causing. He loved playing with the minds of the stupid, greedy humans. That kind was so easy to manipulate. Such fun to watch the results. For once, his superior should be pleased with him. Maybe Azaziel would even move him up a rank.

"I didn't mean to do wrong." The young woman's voice broke, as Ornis saw her try again to understand what she'd done to offend the man. She was pretty, wore a dress that showed a lot of a shapely leg. Ornis could appreciate a pretty form—male or female.

"You do know."

"I didn't... I meant..."

"You do know," the man repeated. He seemed to be growing in power as she weakened.

Ornis chuckled, glad they could not hear him—Damnation to the humans who could. He preferred those oblivious. So much easier.

"I try to do right."

"But you always do evil, commit sins, tempt the weak." Oh just the right note of righteousness in the large man's voice. He did piety so well—of course, that was his job.

"What can I do to make it right?" The girl's voice sounded desperate and angry at the same time. Ornis planted the thought-- *Why was it always my fault?* He saw it take root, but it'd not help her. Not this time.

"You are worthless. God knows I've tried to help you, but..."

"I'll do what you ask."

"You say that, but you don't."

"Give me another chance. I know that you talk to God. I know you know what is right. I want to fix things."

"Do you really want to make amends?" Ornis grinned as he heard the new note enter the man's voice.

"You know I do." That was when the girl saw the gleam in the man's eyes. That is when she felt fear instead of grief. Ornis saw her desire to escape, but where could she go? This was getting good. Nowhere. After all, how could she escape the one she believed was God's emissary. He chuckled again. Humans were so easy to fool.

CHAPTER 2

Catalina Foothills—Tucson, Arizona

I f he had been using logic, something he prided himself in, Mitch Ford knew he'd not have gone for a run in the middle of July—even after midnight. A storm would have cooled off the night, but the monsoon storms had been bypassing Tucson.

Shifting into his wolf form was probably even less logical, although he saw better in his *canis lupus* form. The scents of the desert at night filled his nostrils. He wasn't hunting, though he knew his companion, Adolph, was off somewhere after a rabbit. Adolph was a hybrid wolf legally speaking. He didn't shift, even if he did have a few other rather unusual traits for a wolf—like being able to understand humans and talk himself.

With sharp hearing he never enjoyed as a human, Mitch heard the sound of someone in trouble. A muffled scream stopped him cold, as he listened for its source. It was coming from a dry wash. When he heard it again, his fur bristled as he headed for the sound—a man molesting a woman wearing shorts.

Mitch growled low and lunged at the same moment he realized the two had changed form. It had been a demonic trap. He stopped his leap and landed on all fours. Running as a wolf had left him with no weapons. As a wolf, the demons could overpower him. He had to morph into his human form and fast-- then he had spiritual tools at his disposal.

Naked, in a crouch, Mitch faced the demons who now looked like cougars, prepared to rip his throat out. He growled low, thrust out his hand and felt the earth's energy, rising up in him, before he threw the plasma bolt at the creatures. One screamed as it hit, while the other lunged at Mitch, diverted by Adolph's leap. The demon used a bolt of light that sent Adolph flying. Mitch turned his and the earth's energy on the second demon, watching as it dematerialized with a snicker. "Another day," the first said and then both were gone.

Mitch turned to his wolf to see if he'd been injured. By then, Adolph was shaking a little but standing.

"Don't do that again," Mitch ordered. "I know you meant well, but I don't want you hurt."

"What were they trying to do?" Adolph asked licking a paw.

Mitch squatted and took hold of the paw. The faint light from the moon made examination difficult—at least not for his human eyes. If he morphed into a wolf, he'd not have the use of his hands.

"It was a trap. I should have been more careful. What happened to your paw?"

"I picked up a thorn."

Mitch ran his finger over the bottom of the paw and felt the offending barb. Getting hold of it between his nails, he pulled it out, then held his hand over the paw and let healing energy flow through him. When he put it down, Adolph stood levelly on it. "Thanks."

Morphing back into a wolf, Mitch set off at a lope for his desert home. Wolves at night saw almost as well as during the day, and he easily wound through the cactus, avoiding the thorns, increasing his speed, until he was flying through the desert. Adolph was right behind him and running with no limp.

Reaching the hacienda, Mitch stopped, heaving for breath, as he released the wolf form and morphed into his human body. He could not say to his real form, as sometimes he wasn't sure which was most real or which he preferred.

Adolph flopped to the ground. "What were you trying to prove, brother?" he asked panting before he went to the fishpond to drink.

Mitch shrugged. "Prove? Did I have to prove something?"

"That or trying to cast something out?" The wolf chuckled as he watched the koi head for the bottom of the pool. "Maybe a demon of your own."

Mitch stalked to the swimming pool and dove in, stroking hard from one end to the other. While he enjoyed shifting into a wolf, his human form was powerful. He worked to keep it that way. He cut through the water and felt the heat leave him. Heaving himself onto the edge of the pool, Adolph came to sit beside him. He petted his companion's fur. Adolph might have some supernatural powers, but he had a very real appreciation of being stroked. He gave off a contented sigh.

"Now tell me," his best friend repeated. "What happened out there?"

While he wasn't sure, one possibility stood out. "The book I suppose. Damn the book. It's caused me nothing but grief."

"You felt you had to write it."

"I should have listened to Nantan. He told me it'd draw to me what I didn't want, that it was like a challenge."

"That wasn't how you saw it."

"No." He drew in a breath. "I thought it would help people understand better what they feared, that more was here than they knew. It did not work out that way. They saw instead a superhero to fix their problems." He let out an angry breath.

"Well, you can't undo it."

"No." Much in life could not be undone—like his White Mountain childhood. With an unknown father and his mother dying at birth, his mother's father, Chalipan Ford, had raised him. As a half-breed, Mitch learned he would be fully accepted by no community—which led to loneliness but also an inner strength he hadn't understood, until years later.

His life had a way of changing and it did at the age of six. He had run up a nearby ridge to look down on his grandfather's home. He'd been startled when a figure materialized in front of him. "Boy," the apparition had said, "what do you want most in life?"

He supposed he should have been frightened. Instead, he stood tall as he could. "Who are you?" he had asked rather than answering the old man, who was dressed in full Apache regalia.

"I am your great grandfather."

"Why are you here?" His great grandfather had died years before his own birth.

"Do you want to be a warrior?'" the spirit had asked. Mitch did not have to consider that answer. He nodded.

"The path is not easy."

At six, he had not understood all that meant but answered confidently, "Yes, I want to."

"The cost will be high."

"I don't have money."

"Not that kind of cost." The old man had chuckled. He had settled onto a boulder studying Mitch until he felt uneasy. He then began to talk, to tell Mitch of his own childhood when the Apache way still existed and how it was changed by the white man's invasion. He had explained that he was one who knew the old ways, the legends, and had lived long enough to see the new world where Apaches were forced to adapt to a world they had not chosen. "Do you understand the way of the warrior is about more than fighting?"

He had thought that was all it was about. "I don't know."

"Good answer, young one."

"I am not whole Apache," Mitch had said, trying to keep his voice from breaking.

Yet, you are pure in the ways that matter."

Mitch remembered feeling himself swell with pride. From that day forward, he had a trainer. The years of intense teaching had been whenever he wasn't in school and lasted until he was eighteen—when his life changed again. That was the day his grandfather told him he was dying, and revealed the secret he had withheld—where his birth father lived. Nantan had continued being with him through those years, coming to him when he needed him-- until...

"You are looking too deep, my friend," Adolph said, nuzzling his side, "and taking too much on yourself."

Mitch stared into the starry sky. "Usen," he whispered, "have you forgiven me for revealing your secrets?"

"Not like he'll answer you," Adolph said. "Gods cannot be bothered with useless guilt."

"Useless is it? I didn't need to write the thing."

"You didn't?"

Rising, Mitch walked to where he'd dropped his shorts and pulled them on. "It's caused me nothing but grief. I had plenty of money from what my birth father left me."

"It wasn't about money and you know it."

"No, it wasn't."

"Quit beating yourself over it. It's done, and it was meant to be as it was."

"I doubt that."

The wolf chuckled as only he could. "No, you don't."

Buck Miller, Mitch's right-hand man, came out onto the patio. "Luke Oliver called while you were on your run."

"Kind of late for calls."

Buck shrugged.

"Emergency?" He hadn't looked at a clock but guessed it to be around two. He pushed wet hair back from his face and fastened it with a leather strap. It was shoulder length. Perhaps he should have it cut, but he liked being able to pull it back and out of the way. He cared little about *should*. Maybe that was another mistake.

"Didn't sound like it."

"A problem with Ranger?" He didn't have a barn at his desert home and had been stabling his gelding at the Circle C for specialized training. Damn, the horse better be okay.

"He would have said if it was. Are you taking Ranger when we head north?"

"I hadn't decided." He had more room to ride at his Verde Valley ranch. When he had first bought the chestnut, he'd kept him up there. Whether it was his own wolf energies or just the horse's jitteriness, he'd brought him to Oliver hoping to get the gelding past bucking at anything that frightened him—and pretty much anything seemed to do that. He wanted to be able to ride with Adolph and that had been less than successful.

At the outside bar, Mitch poured himself a whiskey, foregoing the ice. He sat on one of the stuffed chairs around the pool and stared at the desert beyond. An owl called from a mesquite and beyond another answered. The scream of a hawk split the night. His stretch of desert had at one time bought him peace.

He wasn't sure from where the attacks had come, but this one hadn't been the first. To this point, they'd all been when he came to Tucson. He didn't like being run out of Tucson and wasn't sure the Verde Valley would soon prove safer. He loved Arizona, with the kind of love that went deep in a man's soul. It was where his ancestors were buried, most in secret graves.

As he sipped the hard liquor, it hit with a jolt to his belly. He hadn't been drinking much, and he was getting the impact of the alcohol a little more than he might've expected six months earlier. Maybe fasting wasn't such a good idea. He'd take care of that in the morning.

Adolph lay near but said nothing. He knew his wolf wasn't happy with him. Despite his own foul mood, he wanted to smooth the waters. "I know you meant well."

"I don't like it when you are moody."

Mitch ground his teeth and took another sip of the liquor. "It'll pass."

"You need a good fight. Why don't you go down to the bar and..."

Mitch put up his hand. "I do not need bruises." He'd had enough excitement for the night. "You relax, and maybe I will."

"It's not my fault you've been like a grizzly at anything that happens. Maybe you need a woman," Adolph suggested.

Mitch snorted. That was the last thing he needed. Before he could continue arguing with his wolf, he heard the house phone ring. He ignored it. When it shut off, he heard Buck's voice-- not what he was saying. He could have tuned himself to catch the words, but he'd learn soon enough.

Buck came to the door, but before he could say anything, Mitch said, "Pour yourself a stiff one. You look stressed."

"You haven't been easy to work for lately," Buck said taking his suggestion. He came to sit in one of the other lounge chairs. "It was your stepbrother. I figured you were gone."

"He say what he wanted?"

"No. He hung up when I said you were out. The number he called from was not his cell. I think the Holiday Inn out on Oracle. That means you will be hearing from him. I'm surprised he'd call at two thirty. What kind of hours does he keep?"

"I know nothing about his habits. He's not my stepbrother since his mother and my blood father divorced before I even met my father."

"Well, he milks it as much as he can. That story he sold to the tabloid about you being a recluse who he feared was suicidal, that one probably earned him a few bucks along with the telephoto shots he got. Fortunately at a distance, but he's as bad as paparazzi."

Mitch snorted. "Yeah, he's a winner. Any money I give him is soon lost to drugs or whatever else he buys."

"His mother still in Beverly Hills?"

Pouring himself another shot, Mitch said, "I have no idea where Regina is. The witch maybe got on her broomstick and flew to Paris for the season." He chuckled at the image. His father's ex-wife had as little use for him, as he did for her.

"When are we heading north?" Buck asked. "You're always in a better mood on the Verde."

"I have a few business details to take care of, see if Ranger is improved, and then hell yes, soon as possible."

"Any I can help with?"

"Meeting with the accountant," Mitch said with disdain. He didn't blame Jack Ayers for his anal way of approaching everything. It was an accountant's job, but it didn't make any meeting enjoyable.

He looked then to the tallest of the nearby saguaros. At first, he thought a hawk had landed on it, and then he knew better. He had a visitor. "Buck, why don't you head for bed. I will be a while out here."

Buck gave him a curious look but slugged his whiskey and left.

"You want me gone too?" Adolph asked.

"Just stay behind me." He skirted the pool and walked into the open desert where the large bird watched him. He felt a mix of anger and curiosity. "What do you want?" he asked when he stood at the foot of the saguaro.

"What makes you think anything?" The bird flew down and quickly morphed into a human form—not a particularly attractive one.

"Don't waste my time, Ornis. You want something. What is it?"

The demon smirked. "Can't we have a friendly visit?" He looked down at Adolph. "How's your hound?"

"Go before I unleash him."

"Like he could hurt me." Ornis smirked.

"Want to try? I can hold you in a human form long enough for him to give it a shot."

For the first time, the demon looked uneasy. "You could do that?"

"Ask and you shall receive." Mitch smirked.

"Not very nice of you."

"Neither was that little show earlier. Want me to blow away your little friends. Next time I won't just disarm."

Ornis snorted. "I was trying to be friendly and tell you something, but you'll know soon enough."

"Then get out of here."

"More than me is coming." He gave one last smirk before leaving.

"Could you do it?" Adolph asked as they walked back to the patio.

"Not sure, but it'd be fun trying." He laughed, as he thought about Adolph taking a good-sized bite out of that skinny butt. The image put him in a good mood for the first time in what felt like weeks. Maybe he would sleep finally.

At first light, he got up, showered and dressed. He smelled the coffee as he and Adolph came down the stairs. Sofia Phelps was in the kitchen and turned to smile as he entered. "What you want for breakfast?" she asked as she poured him a cup of coffee.

"The usual," he said as he took the coffee and sat at the table.

With smooth movements, she turned the flame up under a burner, set the pan on it, got out eggs and broke them into a large bowl, whipping them.

"How long have you worked for me, Sofia?" he asked.

"Ever since Mr. Robert died," she said. Her face turned sad. "Your papa was such a special man." For the many years she had worked for him, Rosa had been dedicated to the man she always called the mister.

"He was."

"I was glad you took me on."

"You were in California then. How do you like working here in Tucson?"

She turned to look at him. "Why you asking me that? You going to fire me?"

He grinned. "Do I look insane? Nobody cooks like you do."

"Then why you asking?" Her accent only now and again showed up. He had upset her without meaning to.

"I am not sure. I guess I've been doing some thinking about what I should do next."

"You maybe won't keep this house?"

Buck came in to hear the last of that. "You moving, boss?"

"I'm restless, Buck, but no, I don't think I'll sell it, but maybe live more of the year on the Verde."

"And us?"

"It'll be whatever you want. I'd need someone to stay here. For now, I'm just talking through my hat. I don't know what's going on inside my head."

While Sofia added more eggs to the bowl and then began cooking them, he went to the cupboard, opened a can of Adolph's food, and spooned it into his silver bowl. The big wolf gave him a look, indicating disapproval, but began eating. He never talked to Mitch when others were around, not even those as trusted as Sofia and Buck. They had seen many things in the years they'd been with him. They never questioned from where the unexplainable things had come. Whether they had ever heard Adolph talking, before they entered a room, they didn't say. There was a lot they didn't say.

An hour later, Mitch called Oliver. "So what's up with Ranger?" he asked knowing he'd not have awakened the cowboy.

"It wasn't about Ranger. He's doing fine although he likely will always be some skittish. I've done what I can to steady him."

"Then?"

"I got a call from Maria."

"Hemstreet?"

"Yep. Her daughter would like to meet you."

He had known the Circle C was a Hemstreet ranch. Once Marcus had been killed, he had no interest in meeting his family. He had seen Maria once at a charitable event but avoided talking to her. He wondered if that would affect his relationship with Luke.

"Nah," Luke said. "It's up to you. I said I'd ask. That's all."

"You read minds?" Mitch asked.

He heard the low laugh. "Just figured it'd be a possible concern. I train horses, and run the Hemstreet spread, but I'm not part of the *family*."

Mitch wondered exactly what that meant. Luke Oliver had always been a bit of a mystery to him. He knew he was a man of the earth, good with horses, and that had been his family heritage. He talked little and got along even with Adolph, when many feared the wolf.

"Glad to hear that," he said. "I was thinking of taking Ranger for a ride tomorrow morning before it gets too hot."

"Okay, I'll have him in the stable as I probably won't be here tomorrow."

Changing into a polo shirt, slacks, and his one pair of good shoes, Mitch drove into town and to his appointment with Jack Ayers, his accountant.

"I was surprised you're working on a Saturday," he said after the obligatory pleasantries and lowering himself one of the leather chairs in front of Jack's desk.

"I don't usually." He handed Mitch the portfolio. "As you can see, your estate has been growing steadily." He gave Mitch time to scan down the figures.

"Then why the request we meet?" he asked, as he put the folder on his knee.

"I had a visit from your stepbrother yesterday morning."

"Interesting. You know, I assume that Roger Butler is no actual relation to me."

"Yes, I do. It was a strange visit. There was resentment in his voice as he mentioned your father had been his stepfather."

"I usually only hear from him when he wants money. He didn't expect to get that through you, did he?"

"No. He was concerned about the size of your estate now. He looked annoyed when I told him that was confidential. Before he left, he asked about a will."

Mitch smiled coldly. "He should have visited my lawyer. He'd be more likely to know about wills."

"I had the impression he had, and Bill was no more inclined than me to satisfy his curiosity."

"In case he returns, you can tell him I do have one. The estate is set up to go to my help, several charities here in Tucson, one my father always supported, and in a trust for the education of White Mountain Apache youths. None of it will gain Roger anything should I have a surprisingly sudden accident."

Jack smiled. "I was thinking you might want to let him know that. Something about him made me think he needs to know he gains nothing if you die."

Mitch let out a breath. "I'll give that some thought. Frankly, I have as little to do with Roger or his mother as I have to."

"Not hard to understand. Families can be bitches." He shook his head and grinned as he rose with Mitch and shook his hand. "What about the winery?"

"You mean who does it go to?"

Jack chuckled. "No, I meant when do I get the case of Syrah 2012 Reserve? I read it won some impressive awards, and I am on Jacques' list with first options to buy."

"The accounting business must be doing well." Mitch laughed thinking the last he remembered 2012 was going to be an expensive wine.

"Well enough. I do enjoy treating myself with special wines, and that is one I know will be limited."

"I'll let you know when I do. You know how vintners are about such things. Very picky, and the one, who dares tell him his business, will find him gone."

Jack laughed again. "I'll be careful. Just don't let him forget me."

"I'll remind him."

"Thank you."

Walking into the broiling sun, Mitch thought about why Roger might've come to Tucson and what the hell was he doing asking questions about his business dealings? He pulled the Silverado into traffic as he thought about the hate Roger's mother, Regina, had for him. She had accused him of cheating her and her son out of any inheritance—never mind the fact she'd gotten a healthy divorce settlement, despite the fact that she'd been unfaithful to his father. Their marriage had been over before Robert learned he had a son.

Having a movie star for a father, especially one as major a celebrity as Robert Flynn, was a mixed blessing. On the one hand, he was proud of what his father had accomplished, but having not known him until he was eighteen, he had never seemed much like a father. He knew he had inherited his physical stature, tawny hair, strong jaw. Despite being half Apache, he showed little of it, unless it'd be that he had olive skin and almost never sunburned.

Thanks to his mother, Roger had led a soft life leaving him with few resources. He had no idea of the training Mitch had gone through as a child, what it was like to do a vision quest, what toughness meant to a desert man. Roger had been nurtured and coddled with no real skills, at least so far as Mitch had seen. Always he'd looked for shortcuts.

At one time, feeling somewhat sorry for him, he had given him money for supposed businesses. The last time he had come for a check, Mitch had told him no. Whether Roger had enough backbone even to plot a murder, Mitch had no idea. It wasn't his problem either.

To the south, he saw the thunderheads building up. Maybe finally they'd get the storms for which the desert was crying out. The world needed a change. His world particularly.

CHAPTER 3

After a thankfully, quiet week-end, Elke looked forward to getting to the shop right up until she saw a small group, walking back and forth and holding signs. This did not look good.

Witches burn in hell was hand-written and carried by a young girl.

An older woman wagged a finger at Elke. "You Hemstreets need to repent and get the demon out of you," she shouted with three other women nodding their agreement.

'Harry Potter was a demon," cried a young boy.

Elke took long enough to read two other signs.

A man or a woman who is a medium or a necromancer shall surely be put to death. They shall be stoned with stones; their blood shall be upon them.

You shall not permit a sorceress to live, Exodus 22:18.

Nothing too original although the stones drawn below the words were an interesting addition. Since Elke didn't see any actual stones, she held onto her smile, walked past, turned the key, and walked into the shop—locking it behind her.

Torre had arrived ahead of her. "I came in the back," she said as she handed Elke a cup of iced coffee. "What do you suppose this is about?"

"That's what I was wondering. We've had peace for years. Why now?"

"You think it relates to those murders with the women in the crucifixion poses? I mean they never really did charge a murderer. It's only been a couple of months."

"Could be, if someone is out there saying a witch did it."

"Well, it was a sorcerer or a *wantabe* anyway." Torre smiled. They had taken care of the murderer by removing his power, but not in a way that could be explained to anyone. They sat in the office contemplating how long the demonstration would last, and whether it would be the end of their fledgling business.

"Have you heard about someone encouraging this in Tucson?" Elke asked. She told Torre about the young woman who had supposedly sought a spell. "Whether she was actually a reporter or what she claimed, she said she'd heard about us on the street. The question is who would be saying such a thing?" Who gained power by starting such rumors?

"It's not like any of my friends would be likely to hear," Torre said. "I could ask around."

"Do you know anyone who would know?"

She saw Torre considering. "One possibility. He's a street preacher, who works with the homeless, does not have a church that I know of. He might hear such talk. He'd definitely not be behind it though."

"I wonder if Black Cat is getting it too." She rang the bookstore. Devi answered.

"Are you being picketed?" she asked.

Devi laughed. "Not paying high enough wages?"

"Very funny. No, it's the moral police." She told her then about the young woman's request.

"That's odd." Devi hesitated. "Yesterday we did have someone come into the bookstore looking around, and when I asked if I could help, he said he was looking for books on creating spells or making potions. I said no, but suggested a few titles on the history of paganism and asked if that would help. He looked at me strangely and left."

"What did he look like?"

"Bland sort of guy, nothing special about him other than…"

"Yes?"

"Just something in his eyes. It made me glad I refuse to carry books by wantabe witches. Bad juju."

"Do you have *Vislogus*?"

"No choice on that. I mean it's a bestseller, but in fiction, of course." She gave a little laugh. "So what's going on with the pickets?"

"Out front are about ten people, including two children with signs and a vendetta regarding the Hemstreet witches."

"Uh oh."

"Did you happen to get the name of the man who asked for the books?"

"No but he gave off a bad vibe. Not like a sorcerer though."

"If he comes back, see if you can find out who he is."

"Will do."

When she hung up, she looked at Torre with a smile. "It's not like I totally disagree with those people."

"How do you mean?"

"I also disapprove of necromancers," she said in a pious tone. "Those who use demons or even human spirits for evil purposes."

"It is what those people out front think we do."

"It's ignorance. They need to learn what good spiritual power is."

"Oh right, like nobody has tried."

"Have you read *Vislogus*?"

"I heard you mention it just now. Sounds like a chest rub." She chuckled.

"Very funny. *Vis* means power and *logus* is logic. It's an adventure fantasy book, rather like Harry Potter, I suppose."

"That bunch out there don't think much of Potter."

"It's ignorance. Like that word necromancer. Most of the ones who see the word don't know what it is. It's about using the *other* side for evil. We don't do that. We don't deal with shamans who do that either. Yet the word sorcery scares people. It's the ignorance."

"Well, it's in the Bible."

"Along with stoning disobedient children and not eating shellfish or pork."

"Now that I think about it, I do remember a review on that book. Sort of a fairy tale for adults."

"If you don't know it is reality."

"Aren't they making a movie about it?"

"It should be a movie or maybe..." She again thought of the small theater group, whose productions she was helping to support. "Maybe we need a play right here in Tucson that helps people understand spiritual power can be bad or good, that we need the good guys to fight for us because bad spirits exist."

Torre laughed. "They have that part down except in their version, we are the bad ones."

"Only because of that ignorance."

"Believe what you want. I think there's way too much history where witches are regarded as evil to change minds."

"What about that television show from a long time back —*Bewitched*," Elke argued.

"And something like that can turn around people like those outside, who'd love to tie us to a pole and burn us alive? I don't think so."

"*Vislogus* has been a very popular book." When the phone rang, she picked it up. "So what time can I meet him?" she asked without waiting for her mother to say more than hello.

"He said no. He does not want to meet you. Sorry. I tried."

Elke gave a low growl. "He hasn't even heard my proposal."

"And does not want to."

"Who asked him? You didn't tell me your source."

"It won't do you any good. He said no. He's been stabling his horse out at our ranch, and Luke has been training him."

"Then doesn't he owe us a favor?" She was determined. If she got a chance to talk to the writer, she knew she could convince him. A small theater production and maybe then he'd find a way to get a meaningful film done that didn't lose the whole message of his book.

"I won't use that, dear," her mother said with *that* tone, which said she'd not be changing her mind.

"Do you have his address? I could write him." Of course, she had no idea of simply writing him but...

"I am not naïve. Sorry but I won't help you with this."

Elke let out a frustrated breath as she clicked her phone closed. "She won't help me."

"I heard. Why do you want his address?"

"You know why."

"*Vislogus* is a Verde Valley winery."

"How do you know that?"

"If you paid more attention to the best wines, you'd know it too. Its vintner is Jacques Durand. He's world famous."

"I'll take your word for it."

Torre laughed. "It would be highly unlikely that the same names are coincidence. There are listings of who owns which businesses and often addresses."

"You are brilliant."

"I know."

Torre opened her computer and began typing. Elke came to look over her shoulder. "This is a business address, not a home unless his name is Jack Ayers," Torre said as she came to an address.

"No, it's Mitchell Ford."

"I know Jack actually, now that I think about it. I don't think he'd tell us his client's address. He might tell him you would like to talk to him about a proposal though."

"I think we already went that route. I need to talk to Mr. Ford in person."

Torre laughed. "Using your feminine wiles."

"Of course not, but I can be more persuasive when it's face to face."

"I could try with Jack but…"

"I could find him by using extrasensory, but that might get me in trouble. Mom always said never for a selfish purpose. Is this a selfish purpose?"

"I could see it being thought of as to benefit us. Have you done a search for him online?"

"Of course. For some reason no photos. The closest someone got to him was a tabloid article. The photo was at quite a distance and fuzzy, not a recognizable face. It said he was reclusive. His anonymous *friend*, in what served as an interview, feared he was depressive and suicidal."

"That's not good. But then you said a tabloid."

"Two things make me wonder. Friends wouldn't do an article for a tabloid, which means the story is suspect. Then why no real photographs of the guy? He's a famous author. Why wouldn't there be at least a professional photo on the back cover of his book?"

Torre giggled. "Maybe he's a little old man, and it would ruin the mystique of the book."

"Mom said she's seen him. He's tall, but she said little beyond that. The way he looked toward the camera, half crouched, it was as though he was being stalked and didn't like it. Whoever shot the photo only got two images, and at such a distance, they wasted their film."

"The tabloid didn't think so."

"He writes a bestseller and avoids everyone. It makes him of interest, I guess."

"I have a feeling he's about to be stalked again."

"For a good reason though, not just idle curiosity." She wasn't about to add that the one she wanted to stalk was Adolfo Lupan. She finished off her coffee. "I guess we should open up. I'll think about it. Tonight, I meet with David Jefferies at the theater. I'll see what he thinks about a play before I go further pursuing it."

"Why don't you head for the winery? I mean it's got Verde Valley addresses for its vineyard, wine tasting, and purchasing wines. Maybe he's up there now. I mean as hot as Tucson is, who wouldn't be, if they had someplace cooler."

She considered that. "It's possible I could go there. I need to talk to David about the idea first. Maybe he won't go for it. I help support the productions, but there are no strings attached. The next play is scheduled for October, and he may already be set on it."

"You sound like you are having second thoughts."

"No." She went to the door and unlocked it for any customers brave enough to go through the demonstration—although she imagined the heat would not have the protestors there much longer.

"You think we should close until September?" she asked Torre. They certainly didn't get many customers in the heat, and the monsoons, if they ever arrived, would lead to flooding and even less customer interest in buying clothes.

"If you are open to remodeling."

"Do we have the money?" Their original idea was that the shop would pay for any improvements.

"For what I had in mind. Not big things but better flow. Sure."

"We could also work more for Mom in the detective agency."

Torre laughed. "True. While people lose interest in buying nice clothing during the hottest days, the crime rate often goes up with the temperature."

"Then we are agreed."

"And it's not about escaping the witch burners."

"Maybe some. I'd like to know what led them to us. Who could be spreading the word? It is not as though we advertise witchcraft for sale." She gave a little laugh.

"You think a play that is about the supernatural world will help or make it worse?" Torre gave her one of the looks only she could produce.

Actually, Elke had no idea, but she felt something had to happen. She heard the first crack of thunder from south of Tucson. "Guess that will disperse our protestors," she said with a grin as the sky darkened.

"Not if they have faith." Torre giggled.

Walking into the restored building, converted into a small theater and meeting rooms, Elke saw David Jefferies, Pamela Crosby, and two women she didn't recognize sitting at a table on the stage. "You're late," he said as he rose and gave her a hug.

"I'm sorry. Torre and I got involved in planning the changes we want to make in Mellow Yellow, and I lost track of time."

"Nothing major I hope," Pam said dusting Elke's cheek with a brushed kiss before sitting back down. "I love your choices as they are." Considering she did costuming, Elke appreciated the compliment.

David introduced Elke to Debbie Johnson and Colette Ames. "Colette has been in several local productions. Debbie hasn't had any big roles but she seems promising. Chuck was supposed to be here tonight. Not sure what happened to that." Debbie, pretty, blonde and bubbly, was the age to play ingénues while Colette looked a little older than Elke.

"Chuck?"

"Charles Carter. He's been a leading man in several local productions. I had hoped to interest him in our little theater."

"And you succeeded," a tall, rather handsome man, in a sort of bland way, came into the auditorium. As soon as he got to the table, she knew he'd been drinking and not just a little. He looked over at Elke. "Wow, is this beautiful, long drink of water your new actress. If so, I'm in."

While Pam chuckled, the younger actress' disdain for Elke showed on her face. Although Elke had learned to control invading people's thoughts, this didn't take magick to see.

"I'm one of the backers," Elke said with a polite but cool smile. "And interested tonight in what is being planned for fall productions." She looked back at David. "Do you already have something firm for October?"

"Actually I had several plays I was considering depending on the casting call."

"Are you open to something unique?" She wouldn't try to force it based on her donations, even though she knew they helped keep the theater afloat.

"Like what?" David asked.

Chuck settled into one of the chairs not taking his eyes off Elke.

"Have you read *Vislogus*?" David shook his head.

"I have," Pam said. "I loved it."

"Me too," Colette said. "Wow, that Adolfo. What a hero."

"I like playing heroes," Chuck offered. "I might be interested with the right heroine." He raised his brows suggestively at Elke.

She looked back at David thinking if Chuck got out of line, he might be learning a few lessons he hadn't counted on. Being well-trained in martial arts, she wouldn't even need a plasma bolt to do it.

"*Vislogus* is about using magick to combat evil. The hero is a loner for the most and almost a sacrificial figure, who finds most don't understand him."

"Magick?" David said with some skepticism in his voice. "How would that work into small theater? Sounds more like a film with special effects."

"It's the dialogue that would work. It would not require the whole book but several of the chapters are conversational involving the question of using magick. It is the conflict between the hero and the woman he wishes loved him-- but she doesn't. I suppose there is a little of Superman in it, but the dialogue is witty, fast moving and delves into the meaning of life."

"Just two characters?" Colette asked.

"In the book, but it could easily be worked into more for a play— maybe a friend of one of them or even a competitor for the woman's love."

"It's deep?" David asked.

"Not too deep to be confusing but yes."

"And it's a best seller? That's not the usual for Americans."

"Well I suppose the rest of it-- the action is why it's found such favor. The thing though is part of it could be a very thoughtful play with the way it pulls the reader and would a viewer into the questions of life. When Adolfo is threatened, it's mostly because of what he is doing for those who don't understand what he stands for."

"*Avengers* style?" Chuck asked slurring the words a little. "I could get into this."

Debbie glared at him. Elke wondered if the two had something going. It seemed obvious that at least Debbie wanted there to be. Perhaps she'd been misled, as Elke had no sense that Chuck was the loyal type.

"Do you have a copy of the play?" David asked sounding a little more interested.

"Not yet. That is the problem at this point. I could get the play written rapidly because it would practically write itself. I need though to get the author's permission."

David let out a breath. "Who is it?"

"Mitchell Ford. Do you know him?"

"I have heard the name. I am trying to think of why."

"He owns the winery Vislogus in Verde Valley if that helps."

"I know that wine," Chuck said with a grin. "Good wine."

David smiled. "Let's talk about this, after we break for the night." He went through a few of the problems in the theater, discussed when they'd have to have a firm play and finally suggested they meet again August 4th.

When it was just the two of them, he asked, "Is Chuck going to be a problem?"

"Can you count on him in a production? He was pretty well soused tonight."

"I'll decide when we meet again. Maybe it was a onetime thing. He was pretty attracted to you. I hope he won't give you a bad time."

She smiled. "Don't worry about that."

"Back to the question of Ford-- my brother, Bill, had a gathering last winter for those who support Fishing for Loaves. Are you familiar with it?"

"I've heard of it but haven't been involved. I think Mom has been though."

"Well, the gathering was put together by Bill for those who donate to it and for its founder, John Donovan, to explain the work, how the money is being used to not only help with sustenance but also to get people jobs and off the street. Mitchell Ford was there. I had nearly forgotten about it. He didn't say much. If I remember right, my brother is his lawyer."

"Was Martin there?" she asked remembering that David and Bill's brother had his own ministry.

"No."

His answer was clipped. She understood families could be that way. "I want to meet Mitchell Ford and discuss using part of his book. I've had a hard time getting an address."

"I can't promise anything, but I'll see if Bill can set something up."

"If he can't, and I have tried before, think you could get me his address. I know he lives at least some of the year in Tucson."

"I'll let you know tomorrow. Okay?"

"I'd appreciate it. And if you can't, don't worry. This is not connected to the support I have for Stage Left. I will get hold of this guy. If not for an October play, perhaps later."

"I'd have to read the play and know it fit our themes here."

"Give his book a try first." She smiled.

Out on the street, she was almost to her sedan when a figure loomed from the shadow. She wasn't surprised that it was Chuck Carter. "You are really beautiful," he said as he reached for her.

"Nice men don't touch without asking," she said using a quick movement of knee and hand to throw him off balance and onto his back. He lay looking up at her.

"That wasn't nice," he said again slurring his words.

"It gets less nice-- if you touch me again."

She got into her car and drove off hoping she'd seen the last of him. She definitely didn't want him playing Adolfo. The book didn't really describe him, but he was a powerful man, in control of himself in all ways, with what sounded like a rugged countenance. Definitely not the soft Chuck Carter.

In the morning, Elke sipped coffee on her balcony as she considered plans for her day. The remodeling wouldn't start for a few weeks, and Torre would manage that with only the request that Elke stay out of it. It was already too hot for a run. The storm clouds had again built and moved on past Tucson, but she saw the potential for an afternoon storm to the south. They needed the rain. She relished the idea of a powerful lightning storm.

When her cell phone rang, she saw it was David. "Good morning," she said.

"I talked to Bill, and he won't give me the address."

"Thanks for trying."

"I though can tell you this much-- if you are familiar with going out Skyline and beyond the Ventana Canyon trail, there is a big home on the hill overlooking the next draw."

She had hiked that trail in the spring. "I remember that."

"The house is up a long driveway and the gate has a wolf on it." She could hear the smile in David's voice.

"Thank you."

"Don't mention it and believe me, don't mention it."

She laughed.

"I like the idea of the play. I got hold of the book and read half the night. I saw what you were talking about. It'd be exciting and maybe give people some ideas about life not being quite so simple as some believe."

She wondered, not for the first time, if he knew she was a witch. Despite street talk, the Hemstreets had tried not to get publicity for what they did. Their detective agency was run mostly as one. It didn't require magick—even if sometimes that made it easier.

"I won't let anyone know how I got there," she said.

"He might have guard dogs. A lot of people up there have security systems; so if you get arrested…"

"I know. I didn't hear of it from you. I got it from the street." She laughed.

"Exactly."

Putting away the phone, she thought about how to approach this stranger. Doubtless, he had experience with stalkers considering the fame of his book. She didn't want to end up arrested for trespassing. This would take some thought.

By late morning, Elke had created a short outline of her proposal, written two pages of a possible play based on the section she wanted to use. In the folder, she included a pamphlet on Stage Left, what it accomplished and its purpose.

Even though it was going to be a scorcher, she dressed in a white cotton suit with a sleeveless, turquoise, silk blouse to look as professional as possible. She would convince him that he could help others by allowing it to reach new people. She slipped on white sandals, grabbed her bag and headed down the stairs.

"Hello again, beautiful," Chuck Carter said leaning against her car and watching her as she walked to it.

"You are in my way," she said.

"I wanted to apologize."

"Of course, you do. Thanks. Now be gone. I am busy."

"How about dinner?"

"Listen and get it straight. I want nothing to do with you on a social level."

He let out a breath. "And you'll block me from being in that little play of yours?"

"I don't have a play yet, but no, that choice would be the director's, not mine. When we have a script, he can figure that out."

He moved away from the car. "Sorry I tried to grab you last night. I was drunk."

"I noticed."

"Anyway... have a nice day."

"Thank you." She got in her car and drove off, noting in her rearview mirror that he hadn't moved. She hoped he'd not try to get into her apartment. She had it protected with an earth ward, but she was beginning to lose some faith in her ability to cast wards. Hers seemed more effective against spirits than humans. She needed to practice. She thrust him from her mind. A minor annoyance. She would stay focused.

Driving north, she practiced what she would say to Mr. Ford. She hoped she'd get a chance to say something. In her mirrors, she saw the darkness of an approaching storm. Not the greatest day to attempt a meeting, when she might have to walk from a locked gate to the house. From what she recalled of its location, it was set in a forest of saguaros, with no neighbors. He was right under the ridge. She wasn't sure, but it could be as far as a quarter of a mile on a winding drive. She should have worn her running shoes and shorts.

Turning off Sunrise, she turned twice more before she saw the described gate and a curving drive. Beyond, she could only see the upper levels of the house. It looked Moroccan and sat nicely in the huge natural, stone pillars surrounding it—perfect for a recluse.

The wind picked up as she parked. On one of the tall brick posts, there was an intercom. Nothing ventured nothing gained. Far to the south, she heard a crash of thunder. In an hour or less, the storm would be on her. She'd have little time to convince Mr. Ford of the benefit of letting her come up. The wind whipped her hair when she got out of the car and picked up the receiver.

In a moment, she heard a female voice answer. "May I help you?"

"I would like to talk to Mr. Ford."

There was a silence. "Did you have an appointment?"

"I have a proposal." She saw that there was a camera, which meant whomever she was talking to was most likely observing her—luckily she hadn't worn a full skirt or they'd be getting quite an eyeful. "I think he'll find it of interest."

"I doubt that," a deep male voice said.

CHAPTER 4

B eing a typical male, shapeshifting notwithstanding, Mitch had to admire the beauty standing at his gate. Still, he wasn't buying.

"I have a portfolio to show Mr. Ford," she said, her voice a little husky, just the tone he liked in a woman. From what he could tell of her figure under the light suit jacket, the rest of her was too.

"You a reporter?" he asked realizing he was tempted.

"Definitely not. I understand Mr. Ford wants privacy. This is a proposal that I would like him to consider."

Something about her seemed familiar. He wondered if he'd met her before. Curiosity killed the cat but... Knowing he'd regret it, he pushed the gate opener. "Drive around to the side of the house, turn it around, and aim your car downhill since it looks like we're in for a blow." He liked her smile and that walk as she returned to her Mercedes and got in. Nice, he thought.

"Thought you said no," Adolph said with a wolfish smirk.

"Man can change his mind." He gave a little laugh. He hadn't had a woman in a long time. He didn't count the months or years, but it had been too long. Of course, he was sure the proposal this woman had for him wouldn't change that. Why did she seem familiar?

In moments, she had parked the car and found her way to the door that Buck opened for her. "Are you Mr. Ford?" she asked pushing hair out of her eyes.

"No, he's not." Mitch stood at the top of the stairs. "Come on up to the living room, and let's hear this proposal."

He saw the shock in her eyes. He came as a surprise to most people with his large size, muscular build, which with t-shirt and shorts was more obvious than he might've chosen when meeting someone who looked like the woman walking up the stairs. She was a lady, that much was evident. Long, dark hair waved past her shoulders.

When she came level with him, he was a head taller. She didn't look intimidated.

"You uh weren't what I expected," she said. "I am Elke Hemstreet."

"Marcus was your father?" he asked. Not a big surprise she'd be tall and look like a powerful woman. Also no wonder she'd looked familiar.

"You knew my father?"

He wasn't about to tell her how. "An acquaintance. I had a few business dealings with him. I don't do development work though, if that's your proposal."

"No, it isn't." She glanced then around the room. He let his gaze follow hers. The home was eclectic with leather sofas and chairs, Navajo rugs, Hopi pottery, sculptures, paintings of Arizona as well as dynamic abstracts.

"You have a Beringer," she said studying the large impressionistic painting of a woman sitting on a boulder looking out over a vast expanse.

"I remember now. It was in the paper. Your sister just married him, didn't she?"

"She did. I don't have one though." She smiled. "My apartment is too small for them. This room though is perfect."

"I like their energy, and in a practical sense, his colors work well with this room and the desert beyond." He gestured toward the view out the large windows.

"My God, that is a view to die for." She walked to the window and stared at how it framed the boulders and beyond the mountain.

When Mitch had inherited the home after his father's death, he had remodeled it and the window was his addition. Maybe it was the Apache in him, but he couldn't handle feeling closed in.

"Would you like to talk on the deck?" he asked. "We are protected from the wind at least until the storm reaches us."

She nodded and followed him through large French doors. He gestured for her to take a chair. Beyond was the large swimming pool, protected by the boulders, with the trail that led up into the mountain. He liked how his pool looked more like a desert pool than a swimming pool, imagined how she might look swimming in it. Foolish man.

"So you said you had a proposal," he said as he settled in the chair across from hers. Adolph followed and settled at his feet. She watched the wolf.

"Is he a wolf?" she asked, not seeming intimidated.

"Hybrid."

"He looks very pure."

"Of course, I could not have him if was." Mitch smiled.

She didn't look as though she believed him. "Whatever the case, he's a gorgeous animal."

"He is that. Would you like a glass of wine?" She smiled again and he felt an unwelcome surge within. This woman was a risk for him.

"I'd love one. White?"

He pressed a button. "Sofia, could you bring us two glasses of chardonnay?" He turned back to his visitor. "May I call you Elke?"

"I would like that." Again, her tone was soft, a little deep for a woman. There was a sultry quality to her as she crossed her legs, not showing more leg than was modest and yet... all he could think about was those long legs. "Is it Mitchell, Mitch, or Mr. Ford?"

He laughed. "Mitch."

Sofia came out with a tray, two glasses and a decanter. "Will you be wanting anything else?" she asked looking with interest at Elke.

"I'll let you know."

Elke rose and put out her hand. "I am Elke Hemstreet."

Sofia smiled and took the hand. "Sofia Phelps."

When they were again alone, Elke said, "I am trying to think how to start. First of all, I loved your book."

"Thank you." So maybe she was a reporter after all and had lied.

"It had depth, truth, and yet was exciting, full of action. I guess you have heard all that."

He caught himself watching the moisture on her full lips as she sipped the wine. He needed to get a handle on this unnatural attraction. He'd been around beautiful women, and nothing like this had happened. He didn't like it and had to resist the frown that was threatening to take over his face. He didn't want to scare her off and knew his rugged features had a way of doing that—even without a frown.

"It's always good to hear it again," he said, not meaning it. Now he wanted this meeting done. He heard the crash of thunder, and the sky lit up. "We should go in," he said taking the decanter and his glass. With Adolph as his side, he ushered her into the living room just as the sky cut loose, and the rains poured down.

"What a wonderful storm." She stood at the window watching as the rain drove into the pool. The thunder again crashed. At the same time, he saw the bolt hit the mountain.

"We needed the rain." He was making idle talk until he could ask her to leave after the storm passed.

"Now, back to my proposal." She handed him the folder she'd been carrying. "More or less you can see what I would like to do along with information on our small theater."

"Wait, you want to use *Vislogus* in a play?" He didn't like the sound of that.

"Just a few chapters."

"I have turned down movie producers, who have offered me more money than I am sure your theater ever could. I am not interested in seeing it made into a play."

"We weren't planning to offer you money."

He laughed. "Then even more reason to say no."

"Would you read the proposal and about the theater and then we can talk?"

He stared at her considering his options. The longer with her, the harder it might be to say no. "All right." He sat on one of his large leather chairs and opened the folder. The small theater sounded good. Creative, attempting to merge original thinking and entertainment, while providing a place for the actors to practice their craft. All very well but…

He read the sample script using the portion of the book where the argument was made as to from where spiritual power comes and why it needs to be used. It was well done and cleverly integrated dialogue into a challenging scene, inventing a third character, who represented the spirit guide in the scene. It didn't change his mind. He had reasons. He looked up, and she was watching him.

"You have a stake in this, I take it."

"I wrote that scene, but I am not the director. That would be David Jefferies."

"Small world."

"It can be." The thunder crashed seemingly overhead shaking the house.

"And his brother is how you got my address."

"That would be my secret. There are other ways than using your lawyer."

He chuckled. "But not in this case. I value my privacy. I am careful who I let know where I live."

"You are limiting an important work, which could reach more people if you were open to sharing it."

"I wrote the book. That was enough."

"Do you know Adolfo Lupan?"

He laughed then. "So that's what you really want."

She flushed. "Well... I did hope to meet him."

"What made you believe he was real and not fictional?"

He saw her consider that. She was in no hurry to answer, which made him believe her real motives in all this were way more complex than she was about to tell him.

A lightning bolt flared blindingly, as it struck the boulders outside his home. He turned with Elke to see a huge red boulder with a black burn mark zigzagging down its surface to the ground.

"I've never seen it do that," she said as she moved to the window.

He knew that hadn't come from nature and grabbed her around the waist pulling her away as he twisted to protect her with his own body just before another bolt struck his window shattering it. He felt pain as shards of glass struck his back.

"Not a good room to be in a storm." He put his arm around her directing her to his more protected den. He expected her to be shaking. She wasn't. Adolph, who had stayed away from the windows in the storm, followed, and settled himself on his bed in a corner of the room

Mitch picked up the intercom and told Buck what had happened. "Call Jeromes and tell them to send out a repairman with glass for the living room." He laughed. "Yeah, you know the one."

"You're bleeding," she said as she moved to study his back.

"Nothing much."

"Glass might be in the cuts. Take off your shirt."

She hadn't asked what happened. Given who her father was, he guessed that should not have surprised him. He unbuttoned his shirt and slid it off his shoulders. He believed the cuts didn't amounted to much. He had been enough distance from the window when the bolt hit. He felt her fingers probing what he knew would be little gashes, most just pinpricks. Only one hurt.

"I've never seen a window do that." She stepped back a little. "This will take warm water, tweezers, soap, towel, and antiseptic cream."

Before she'd gotten out the words, Sofia was in the den with a tray holding the items. The storm was still raging outside. "I can take care of it," Elke said before she turned back to him. "Sit on one of those wooden chairs, and I'll make sure this is clean and no glass." She looked over then at Sofia. "I see a piece in the large muscle here." She pointed. "I think another one... Some whiskey would be good about now."

"Antiseptic cream not enough?" Sofia asked looking a little dazed at Elke's taking over.

"I was thinking for drinking." Elke grinned.

He straddled the chair, leaning his forearms on it, and felt her touch again as she began washing away blood, studying the cuts. When Sofia returned with the whiskey, she handed him the bottle while she pulled two shards.

"It stopped bleeding already," she said as she dried his skin before applying the ointment. "You won't need bandages. You look as though you heal quickly. You expected it, didn't you?"

He shrugged back into his shirt. "Not all of it." While he'd seen something like it before, that kind of playing with lightning was new. If he had expected it, he'd not have taken her into the living room. The thought of her tender skin being pierced by glass was not to be risked.

"I knew your book was not fiction." Her gaze was hard on him.

"If you did, then you also know why it's best it not become a film or play. It... draws trouble to those involved." He picked up the whiskey bottle and took a big swallow.

Elke tried to think how she might get through to him, but she understood all too well his concerns. "You think anyone making it into a film or play would be at risk. Is that what you are saying?"

She looked away from him trying to get a handle on the emotions surging through her. She'd never seen a man as beautifully built. His muscles were long, strong and well-developed. Even with his shirt back on, she kept imagining his chest, the well-developed pecs, that ridged belly. Not smart, Elke, she thought with a wry smile.

"To speak of some things is a risk, yes," he said finally.

"But you did it."

He didn't answer and instead looked out the window to the valley in the distance. The storm was moving north. It hadn't been right over them when the bolt had marked the boulder and another destroyed his window. She had been shocked but understood now what had been wrong with it. No thunder. It had been a covert attack—and not of nature but from the spirit realm.

She saw glasses on a shelf. Got one and took the whiskey bottle from him, pouring herself a shot before she handed it back. She needed it. When she had thought he wouldn't say more, that any idea of getting him to agree to a play was impossible, she moved to one of the leather chairs and sat sipping her whiskey.

In a way, she understood. "Did you interview Adolfo Lupan?" she asked though she knew the answer.

"Sure and he told me the whole thing." His smile was twisted.

She turned then to the wolf who had risen from his bed. "Is that true?" she asked. The wolf's golden eyes shifted between her and Mitch. "Adolph," she added.

"You think he told me the story?" Mitch asked moving to the chair across from her. His smile looked amused.

"Adolph does mean wolf. I just meant that."

"Did you?"

She debated then. She was asking him to trust her but did that mean she also had to trust him? It wasn't that he would not believe her, but she wasn't sure it would gain much either. She decided to go part way with it. "I recently had a woman come to my shop claiming she wanted me to do a spell."

"Claiming?" He was quick to pick up on words and their meaning.

"I wasn't sure about her truthfulness. She could have been a journalist hoping for a story."

He rose, went to the sideboard, took a glass, and poured himself a shot. "Want more?" he asked

She shook her head.

"And you're telling me all this why?" he asked as he settled back into the large chair watching with a speculative gleam in his eyes.

"People misunderstand magick—the real deal, not a trick. We had a group come to our shop and picket it."

"For what reason?"

"Thinking we are witches, evil doers, my sister and I who own the shop."

"Witches don't exist," he said, and this time she knew the gleam was amused.

"Of course not, but some just don't understand that." She put a pious tone to her voice.

"I want to repeat. My book was fiction. Adolfo was imaginary."

"And the bolt that marked your rocks, the one that shattered your double-paned window, they were also fiction and imaginary."

"Just lightning. The risks of living on the mountain as I do."

She put her glass down. "Lightning without thunder."

He shrugged.

"I am sorry for wasting your time. It seems the storm has passed, and I should go." They neither trusted the other, and she would not get his permission to do his play. She did understand his reasons. She'd find another way to get across the truth to as many people as she could. It was important. She had seen his motives were logical. She couldn't even deny the risks about which he was referring.

At the door, he said, "I am sorry I could not help you."

"At least you listened. I appreciate that. Uh, could I ask one more question?"

"You can ask, but not sure if I'll answer." His smile turned hard.

"Do you know Ornis?"

She saw she had surprised him. If he understood magick, then he did know the demon who, at the least, influenced much of the evil done in the Sonoran Desert. If he had any of the spiritual power of which he wrote, he would know Ornis whether he knew his name.

"Is that a painter?" he asked. His crooked smile irritated her and told her he did know the demon but wasn't about to give her anything.

"Of course. Just thought with the Beringer on your wall. Oh well, sorry for wasting your time." She walked to her car and drove down the long drive. The gate opened before she got there and closed as soon as she drove through. She didn't know if Ford watched her drive off.

~

"You weren't very polite to her," Adolph said trotting at Mitch's side as he headed around the house.

"Better that way."

"You know who she is, don't you?"

"She's the daughter of Marcus Hemstreet, who was a powerful wizard and another of my many mentors. Yes, I know who she is. I should not have let her come up."

"Is she active in the craft?"

"I don't know and don't want to know."

Adolph chuckled. "Yes, you do."

"I'm going for a run. The desert smells like rain. It's a good time, and if I see Ornis, I will rip his throat out." He dropped his clothing by the pool and shifted into a wolf. In moments, he was on the narrow wildlife path that he took most often, letting his legs stretch out and the run take over all thought. He dug his nails into the wet sand and leaped over the bare bones of a fallen saguaro. He imagined it when it had been a small cactus, what it might've seen in this desert where man had been for thousands of years with constantly changing cultures. Then it grew old and withered into ribs, with the flesh gone. Much as he would be someday... or sooner as things were heading.

If he hadn't known his own life would be short, that he had a price to pay for revealing secrets, which some believed must never be told, he might've pursued the beautiful Elke Hemstreet.

He knew she'd never remember, but he had seen her before. He'd gone with his father, who wanted to talk to Marcus about a building project in which he was considering investing. They'd come to the Hemstreet home and met in a large den. Mitch had mostly been listening to the two men debate the merits of the investment. The girls had come in without knocking, but Marcus had been tolerant of them, smiling as he sent them on their way while he went back to talking business. Even though still a girl, Elke had been the one to catch his eye. The dark hair, straight nose, beautiful, intelligent eyes, and slender build, had all found fruition in the woman.

Before they'd left that day, Marcus had pulled him aside. "There are things you need to know," he'd said.

"I'll meet you in the limo," his father had said with a tolerant smile. Robert Flynn had no mystical powers beyond drawing audiences to want to see every film he made, even as he approached his senior years. He had though recognized Mitch's abilities, the training he had already received from the other side. He had approved and maybe it was even why he'd suggested Mitch come with him that day.

Marcus had told Mitch of the battles to come. "Someday," he had said, the words engraved on Mitch's brain even after all those years, "you will be fighting for your life and possibly being asked to make the ultimate sacrifice." Mitch had said nothing as he wondered why tell him that now. "Because," Marcus had said, "you know it don't you?"

Mitch had nodded.

"You will be a great warrior. I know things that can benefit you and maybe help you go through those years."

"And you want to teach me?"

"More is the case-- must." Marcus had smiled. Handsome as the man was, his smile was even more devastating in its impact on the younger man. He was eager to learn all he could be taught. "I may not have long, "Marcus had said, "so we can't waste time." Mitch had looked at him with curiosity, wondering what that meant, but Marcus didn't say.

They met whenever Mitch got to Tucson. From his great grandfather, he had learned the Apache way. Marcus taught him the warrior way. Robert Flynn's home in the hills was their place for battling with swords. The swords and later bows and arrows used the alloy platinum osmirdium, which when forged by a wizard like Marcus, could destroy monsters and even demons.

Finally, Marcus had said, "I've taught you all I can."

"I like meeting with you."

Marcus had smiled, an enigmatic smile. "We may meet again... someday." When Mitch had learned of the motorcycle accident, which robbed the world of Marcus Hemstreet, he had not met Marcus for a few years, but felt a keen sense of personal loss. It had never been a friendship, but that of master and student.

He wondered if Marcus would have approved of the book, or would he have shared the belief of Nantan Lupan. Perhaps he could have asked, as Mitch knew the spirits of the dead sometimes came back to help others. He didn't ask. It would have been wrong. He had to bear the responsibility for his decision. He most definitely would not put any of it onto Marcus' daughter or his family. He needed to keep Elke Hemstreet a long way from himself. She might be facing humans who accused her of being a purveyor of magick. There was worse out there.

At the top of a ridge, Mitch stopped, Adolph had stayed at his side. The two looked out over the vast desert, the city and then the mountains beyond.

"You are troubled," Adolph said.

"No."

"Do not lie to your friend."

"I'm not. I just was thinking back."

"To her father, I suppose."

Adolph had been with him when Marcus had come in and out of his life. Mitch didn't actually know how old Adolph was, but it had to be old for a wolf. He hoped the supernatural aspect of his wolf would keep him young forever—or at least until Mitch himself crossed over. He grinned his own wolfish smile as he thought that was selfish, but so be it.

"Your thoughts are dark," Adolph said.

"How old are you, my friend?"

"Calculating it in your years... 105 but I am not an average wolf, you know."

"You were not much more than a pup when you came to me."

"Like yourself."

"I want us to grow old together. But I am not likely to grow old. I have painted a target on myself."

"We draw to us what we put out. Do you want to die early?"

"I didn't think so at one time."

"And now?"

"And now, I don't know." He thought about Elke-- and what it might be like to be with a woman like her. He'd never had such a thought before. There'd been women but casual connections with neither wanting more. It didn't matter. He'd not see her again. He would head for the Verde and his vineyard. It would be a better place to defend if this was heading as he believed.

"When do we go?" Adolph asked obviously reading Mitch's mind.

"I need two days. So by Thursday, I guess."

"Not waiting for the new moon."

"No need to wait for it."

"Makes no difference to me." Adolph snickered. "I don't believe in astrology."

Mitch started back down the path. Neither did he. He wasn't sure what he believed in. Maybe nothing. He wondered when that had happened. Maybe it was feeling as though it was a continual battle and nothing ever ended or worked out. Maybe it was realizing if a powerful sorcerer like Marcus Hemstreet could be killed in a fluke, meaningless accident, was there meaning in anything?

CHAPTER 5

Parking in front of her mother's home, Elke saw that everyone else had already arrived. The phone call to meet had come as she drove back from the hill. What could be so important that the circle had been called? Once in the house, she was offered iced tea or lemonade by Celia, her mother's cook.

With a glass of iced tea, she went into the large living room. Her mother and both grandmothers were sitting on the sofa and from the sounds of it had been arguing. Denali was on the chair across from them and gave Elke a smile as she entered. Devi and Torre were standing by the fireplace and had also apparently been in private conversation. The only one missing was Aunt Rosa.

"What is so important?" she asked as she took one of the chairs.

"The demonstrations are growing," her mother said. She handed Elke the newspaper with photos of the protestors only this time at the bookstore. "Apparently, they believe they drove you and Torre out of business, and the Black Cat is next."

"We are just taking a break and making some improvements," Elke protested. Torre nodded as she sat in one of the chairs.

"Maybe so but that's not what they believe."

"Who is behind it?" Denali asked. "Does it relate to the murders?"

"Unsolved murders or so they believe," Elsa, her grandma Hemstreet, said.

"And that started this?" It was impossible to provide a murderer

48

after the justice they had dispersed on Braddock. Perhaps that had been an error.

"An excuse, not a reason," Denali said. "The police are not coming around to question Nick, which means they consider it closed."

"Naturally," Torre said, "leaving the door open for a fanatic to use it."

"You didn't believe we had done wrong at the time," Denali protested.

Torre shrugged. "I didn't know how it would be used by someone."

"And the someone is?" Elke asked. She had spent a rather disturbing day and didn't need more to worry about.

"Most likely the minister who runs the church where these people are coming from," her mother said. "Martin Jefferies has been growing his congregation with brimstone as his fuel. Faith in Action likely needed something more to bring in a lot of money and keep the energy high for his parishioners."

"Why us though?" Elke asked.

"Enemies make for power," Maria suggested.

"Perhaps someone knows what we did to Braddock," Elsa said.

"More he did that to himself by the path he chose," Jess spoke up. Being Maria's mother, Elsa and she had neither been called grandmas. They also rarely agreed on anything.

"That doesn't help much now," Elsa retorted.

"We should not argue among ourselves," Maria said. "I don't know how seriously to take this. It might blow over. I thought we all needed to be prepared and of a same mind, so our energy will be more effective."

"Has Nick painted recently?" Elke asked, looking at Denali, thinking of the work she had seen at Mitchell Ford's home.

"Why would you ask?"

"Because of the ones he did under the influence of Ornis."

Denali huffed. "That did not influence his work? But no, the demon has not bothered Nick, now that he understands what was happening. Nick may not be a wizard, but his skills are also powerful. He blocked Ornis, who is likely off causing mischief elsewhere." She snorted her disdain.

"Good thing one of you girls got that one," Jess said with a wicked smile. "Wouldn't want a man that handsome and talented getting away."

"With Gallery 11 gone, where will he show his work in Tucson, or will he?" Maria asked.

"He and I have been discussing that. I think I found a building that will work. We neither wanted Gallery 11. Too many associations. I will manage the new one for him."

"What will you call it?" Torre asked.

"We don't know yet."

"I think that's a great idea," Elke said. "Where is the building?"

"It was a warehouse, under the shadow of A Mountain. Lots of positive energy and parking. Not that the parking is more important than the energy." She grinned. "We've been talking to an architect. I think it will have room for a lovely gallery space, after we get the lighting right. He will have a studio in the back and maybe some space for classes. He'd be a good teacher if he wants that."

"When are you going to those openings? The ones you bought the dresses for?"

"We leave Thursday but will fly back Monday."

"Mitchell Ford, the writer, had one of Nick's paintings," Elke said before she thought.

"And how did you learn that?" her mother asked with one of those smiles.

"I told you I wanted to convince him to let us make a play out of some of his book. Incidentally, he said no."

"Did he give a reason?" Elsa asked at the same time Torre asked, "What does he look like?"

"He said the book drew negative to it, and he wasn't going to be responsible for it hurting anyone else. And he's handsome, rugged features, dark blond hair, quite tall, and very muscular."

"Yum," Torre said with a grin. "And intelligent enough to write that book to go along with it."

"When you read the book, did you get the feel it wasn't fiction?" Elsa asked. "I had a definite feeling that Adolfo Lupan existed and told his story to Mitchell Ford. Of course, I adored it and would love to see it as a film or a play."

"As things stand, it won't be happening," Elke said.

"Did you tell him why you particularly wanted to do it?" her mother asked.

"Not all of it."

"In other words, he doesn't know you are a witch."

"It's hard to say. We had a rather odd experience while I was there." She described the lightning streaked boulder and then the shattered window. "It wasn't lightning," she said. "I was shocked by the second bolt, so soon after the first, or I'd have put up a protective shield. Mitch got some cuts out of it when he got me out of the way."

Maria grinned. "Sounds very heroic."

"You going to try again to convince him?" Elsa asked with the same grin the others had.

"Maybe but likely it won't work any better."

"If he's that cute, I wouldn't mind trying," Torre said with a laugh. "Just to get his wine at a discount if nothing else."

"I hadn't connected that," Jess said. "He's Vislogus wine then?"

"Yes." It appeared her family were more wine connoisseurs than she—not hard to be, of course.

"We are losing track of our own problem, not that I mind discussing delicious wine or men," Torre said, "but if Martin Jefferies' church is behind our harassment, what is behind him?"

"You mean who?"

"Should one of us visit to check out the services?" Devi asked.

Elke looked at her with surprise, as Devi tended to be the shy one. Was she volunteering to go into a church, which would obviously be very unwelcoming to a Hemstreet given what had been happening?

"I'd go with you," Elsa said with the kind of smile only she could give, half between a shark and a koala bear. Even experimenting in front of mirrors as a little girl, Elke had never mastered it. "I think it'd be fun." Now the smile had turned pure shark.

"You know they might kick you out," her mother said.

"If we went as us." This time it was Devi, who grinned. Of course, they could go as any doppelganger they chose. Unless there were other witches already in the congregation or possibly sorcerers, they would never know.

"Could be amusing," their mother said. "All right, do it. Perfect week-end for it. With the new moon on Saturday and Lammas next Friday. This is a powerful time for a..." She stopped when the phone rang. Elke heard Celia get it.

"Maria," she said, "it's that detective fellow."

Maria smiled and took the phone. She quit smiling as she listened. When she hung up, she said, "We have a problem."

"I heard," Denali said, as Elke knew she often listened to both ends of a conversation. "Another murder of a woman." Her face had whitened and her tone was bleak.

"But the first murderer is incapable of doing it again," Jess protested.

"Copycat would be my guess and whoever did it, didn't know that the original murderer has been incapacitated, which means a human —with no connection to the other side," Denali said.

"What happened this time?" Elke asked when her mother poured herself some wine.

"A young woman, left naked and in the pose of the other two. Jace said they believe she been raped—or at least had had relations with a man before being beaten. The autopsy will determine cause of death." Her mother took a big sip of the wine.

"Do they know who she was?"

"Deborah Johnson. Her purse was beside the body, and nothing had been taken, not even the money in it."

"Debbie Johnson?" Elke felt a chill go down her spine.

"I suppose. Young, pretty, blonde."

"That is so tragic. I was just with her when we discussed the next play. I can't believe…"

"Where was her body found?" Denali asked. Elke could see her concern that they would be coming after Nick again.

"They won't think it's Nick," Torre argued.

"They like things tidy," Denali said with a grimace. "I was with him last night, but as his wife, I don't know how much my word will count."

"You should go home to be with him in case they do come around," Maria said.

Denali rose. "All right, and when you know anything, let us know." With that, she was out the door.

Elke and the other sisters stayed for a late lunch while the grand-mothers left with a promise they would consult their guides.

"Tell us more about Mitchell Ford," Torre said

Before answering, Elke tasted the delicious tomato soup that Celia had made. "Not much to say. He's got a beautiful home. Moroccan style. I was disappointed he wouldn't let the play use a few scenes from his book. I showed him a rough idea of what it would look like. He did read it, but it didn't persuade him."

"He's not wrong about his concerns," her mother said.

"It's what made it complicated."

"So, you've given up."

"No, I'll work to put together the whole play and then go back."

"Maybe he needs to know who you are."

Elke looked up with surprise. "You mean a witch?"

"He would understand better your need to help people understand magick comes in various forms, as does everything else."

"I'll think about it." She wasn't sure it would help.

Back at her home, Elke changed into shorts and a tank top before opening *Vislogus* to the scenes she wanted to use. She had written where Estella was arguing with Adolfo that he was not giving her enough time. When he tried to explain, she cut him off. Estella saw violence as always wrong. Though she didn't appear to know all Adolfo was, she tore into what he had accomplished, forcing him to defend his actions—until he decided his only option where it came to her was to walk away. That scene only needed two people to make an interesting play.

She wondered if Adolfo loved the woman, but they were so different as to make any other choice impossible. Turning the argument into dialogue, she heard the bell from below signaling someone wanted to come up.

At the intercom, she said, "Identify yourself," even as she recognized who it was.

"Detective Myers. I have a few questions for you."

She sucked in a breath but pushed the button to release the bottom gate. She met him at her door. "I heard about Debbie's murder at my mother's. I guess that's why you're here."

He nodded. "I have talked to those who saw her last. David Jefferies mentioned you were one of those."

"I was. Can I get you something cold to drink? I have some lemonade, beer."

"Lemonade would be nice."

She got him a glass and then sat across from him in her living room. "I was in shock. I guess you hear that a lot when someone has just been with someone who was murdered."

"Do you recall who was there?" He took out a notepad.

"Pamela Crosby, who does makeup and costumes. Of course, David and Colette Ames."

"I think I've seen her in some plays. I was though not familiar with Deborah."

"I had the feeling she was new. I'd never met her or Colette. And then Chuck Carter, who David hoped to interest into becoming a leading man."

"I've seen him in some plays."

"Yeah." She shook her head. "She was so young. Maybe not even twenty. Such a tragedy."

"Then I don't suppose you knew any of her friends?"

"Not at all." She thought then of the resentment, Debbie had shown when Chuck had so quickly hit on her. She didn't feel free to mention something so gossipy. Should she tell Jace about how Chuck had tried to grab her? She held off, feeling it might be unfair, after all, he had been drunk. Trying to kiss a woman was not remotely related to murdering one.

"It might be the same killer we had several months ago." He looked glum.

"There was reason to think that?"

"Similarities and differences."

"What about a copycat?" She couldn't tell Jace why she knew for certain it was not the same killer.

"That is possible, of course. Your lemonade is good." He smiled and for the first time Elke wondered if he had come to her as an excuse to probe into whether her new brother-in-law, Nick Beringer, could be a serial killer.

"I am a detective, you know," she said. "If you'd like to bounce some of your ideas off me, I'd be glad to listen and share anything that comes to me."

"I didn't know you still did that after you opened the boutique."

"Less of it, but for now the boutique is closed for... repairs."

"I heard about the protestors. You should have called the police."

"Freedom of speech, you know. They weren't breaking any law."

"It could be regarded as harassment. Such things sometimes escalate, and we could come down and discourage that from happening."

"I will remember that. Uh, I have a question."

"Shoot… figuratively speaking." He smiled again. He was a nice looking man. Not her type but a nice looking fellow.

"Are you familiar with the church, Faith in Action?"

"Yes, congregation of around a thousand, I believe. Martin Jefferies is the pastor. It's an energetic group." He smiled again.

"You know they are the ones protesting."

"I had heard that."

"Have they been engaged in protests before? I hadn't even heard of them until they were outside my door with the signs."

"They have gone after clinics where abortions are performed. Nothing violent though. I think they have tried to bring in other congregations to increase their influence but haven't heard that happened. I don't attend there myself."

"You are a church goer?" She found herself surprised and then felt guilty.

He smiled. "Not regularly, but sometimes I go to the services John Donovan holds south of town."

"I heard about him but haven't met him."

"He has a street ministry. He's a good man, enthusiastic about God and helping the poor. He was in prison and found his purpose there."

Elke had little faith in standard religions, but it did sound like Donovan did good work. Everything she'd heard about the street preacher was all positive.

"Well," she said, "I am hoping that you find the killer of Debbie. Although, I can't say I knew her, she seemed like a sweet girl."

"Did your brother-in-law know her?"

So she had been right. "I haven't ever heard of Nick being involved in small theater. I think he's too busy."

"Probably not. Just thinking out loud."

She bet he was.

As soon as he left, she clicked on Denali's cell.

"What's up?" her sister asked.

"Jace was just here. I think you can expect him if he hasn't already gotten there."

"I told Nick." She let out a breath. "He was sickened, of course. He also was with me all last night."

"I think the police are grasping at straws. Since we know it's not the same man, we also know the police need to look for someone new. They can't know that."

"Thanks for the heads up."

When she hung up, Elke remembered when Chuck Carter had come in and the unhappy look on Debbie's face—followed by the aggressive way Carter had treated her. Had Debbie seen that, leading to an argument? It took her to her original thinking-- grabbing a woman was a long way from killing one.

She took several deep breaths and let her mind return to the meeting in the theater, to all that had transpired. She saw how Carter had ignored Debbie and how her irritation had grown. Maybe she would have to tell Jace. Before she did that, she'd send out feelers to see if the spirit world had anything to tell her. There were rules for how involved they could be, but it never hurt to ask.

Undressing for bed, she thought back then to her meeting Mitch Ford. It was strange how she had felt she'd met him before but that was impossible. She understood his reasons for denying her the rights to use his book. There was no more reason to see him except, she wanted there to be. She'd never met a man who interested her on so many levels. Yes, he was physically exciting, but it went beyond that. His power was of the spirit as well as the body.

It was after midnight when she heard the buzzer to admit someone. There was no way she would be doing that but she got up, threw on a robe, and got the intercom. "Yes?" she asked.

"I need to talk to you. It's Chuck."

"No. I don't know you well enough to let you up here at night."

"Did you hear about Debbie?" His voice sounded shaken.

"Yes, I did. Talk to the police."

"They questioned me."

"Good."

"I think they suspect me of… doing it."

She sent out her energies and felt what was in his thoughts. His mind was dark, angry, and full of turmoil. Fears made it impossible for thoughts to form. If he killed Debbie, he might not even be aware of it, given the way substance abuse clouded minds. "I am sorry," she said, "but you cannot come up."

"I will break down the door. It's flimsy," he threatened.

"I suggest you not try that." She felt no fear, just a strong sense of purpose. If he broke down anything, he'd find himself flat out, with the police on their way.

"All right," he said with a sob, "but you'll be sorry you didn't help me."

"I'm already sorry I know you. Goodnight." She sent out energy again to decide whether he was leaving. When she felt him walk away, she looked out her window. He was stumbling a little. Probably drunk. She hoped he'd not be back, but she suspected she'd not seen the last of him. She would call her mother in the morning and...

The ringing phone interrupted her thoughts. She wasn't surprised at the caller. "What happened?" her mother asked.

"And how do you know anything did?" She smiled, as she knew the answer to that.

"I only put out protections for dangers," her mother said defensively.

"Nice they alert you."

"No point in being a witch if I can't help my own family, now is there?"

"Do you ever sleep?" She laughed.

"Of course, far better when I know the alerts are out."

"Well, tell them thank you. It's fine here. Nothing going on." Now. "Uh, did Myers question Nick tonight?" She tried for a distraction to avoid telling her mother about Chuck. She didn't want her mother worrying. She could handle that situation, but her mother might be less confident.

"No. I think he has decided it's not the same person, and Nick had no motive plus an alibi sleeping with his wife."

"Good. I'm heading for bed. Sweet dreams."

Her mother gave a snort and a little laugh. "You too."

When she hung up, Elke wondered again about Chuck Carter or had it been someone Debbie had met, trusted and had a reason to kill her? Why try to make it look like the earlier murders? As best she knew it, there were several reasons for killing someone. Self-defense didn't fit this situation at all. Debbie might have been blackmailing someone. She could have simply come across the wrong person. The real question was why make it look like the earlier killings?

She thought then of the young woman and how she had awakened that morning with no clue that her life was about to be cut short. She thought about contacting the spirit world, trying to reach Debbie on the other side. That was never a good idea—most especially not with a violent death. Debbie needed time to adjust to what had happened. There were those over there who would be helping her. It was not up to Elke to interfere with the natural process—that was how hauntings happened with spirits unable to release their earthly life.

But there was a murderer, here in Tucson. It was her duty, that of her family to try to find who had cut short the life of the pretty actress. The young woman had been excited and full of life, maybe using poor judgment on which man, with whom she became involved. She didn't deserve what had happened.

Elke shook her head as she stared at the ceiling. So much of life was beyond her ability to grasp. How could she know what the reason had been behind the murder when she saw only a small piece of the pie? As a witch, she saw more than most but still not all. Mystery was the best word for what she had to accept. But not without trying.

In the morning, she would set out to find who traveled in Debbie Johnson's circle. Maybe someone she knew had a motive to end her life. If it was a murder of opportunity, random in that she was in the wrong place when the wrong person came along, there'd be no easy solving of the crime. She had to try. For now she would put aside her interest in Mitch Ford and his book—or try to anyway.

CHAPTER 6

After sleeping poorly, Elke made coffee and considered what steps she needed to take to find a motive—hoping there was one. With the boutique closed, she had time for an investigation. She first needed to find where the body had been left, see photos if possible of the corpse, and then set about researching Debbie's life.

As she dressed in a white sleeveless top and short lavender skirt, she thought of why such a death might've come to the girl. Spiritually there were reasons tragedies were allowed to happen. That didn't mean the murderer should not be held to account. Earth residents, of which witches were among, had the responsibility to keep order. She and her family were committed to that order. The risks they took, the work they did went to their ancestry. She felt proud of her lineage, the stories of other Hemstreet witches. She would not let down those who had come before.

Surprisingly hungry, she scrambled eggs, fried some bacon, and fixed herself a piece of toast to take onto her patio to enjoy the scented, early morning air. She'd have to run the calories off, but it'd be worth it. After she ate, she refilled her coffee cup and returned with a notepad to make a list of what she needed to do first.

"Hon?" Maya called up from the garden.

She looked down. "Hi, how are you this morning?"

"Upset, that's what. Did you read about that poor girl?"

"Yes, I did."

"Paper said it was the same as the other two women. That means Tucson has a serial killer, doesn't it?"

"There are other possibilities."

"She was left the same way. They didn't give her name. Family hadn't been notified, but poor soul, whoever she was." She made the sign of the cross while she mouthed the familiar words and then said aloud, "May she rest in peace."

Tony came out of his condo, which was unusual as he generally didn't enter the garden. The talking must've drawn him. "You talking about the murder?" he asked. He was sipping what looked like tea.

"Yes, we were," Maya said. She shuddered. "Three and maybe some monster out there waiting for another." She looked up at Elke. "I'm too old for that kind to bother with, but you be careful, you hear."

"Of course. You know, this may not be the same killer." She felt she should add that to tamp down the hysteria she felt rising in Maya.

"I thought it said left the same way—didn't say much though about what that was. There's been talk about it on the street."

The street again. "There are copycat killers, you know." For the first time, Elke felt doubts about the first two murders. Could it be possible it had not been Braddock? No, it had been him. Someone had created the impression the new murder was the same for nefarious purposes—the most likely of which would be to stop the police for looking for a motive.

Tony sat on one of the chairs. "You're a detective, right?" he asked looking up at Elke.

"I work for my mother's agency on some cases."

"Have you looked at this one?"

"It hasn't been long enough for us to be asked."

He watched her speculatively. He was handsome enough in a white bread sort of way. She knew he had girlfriends off and on but nothing steady. She could have probed what he was thinking but that would have been rude. Magick had to be wisely used, or it lost power. It was one thing *Vislogus* had also taught. She batted away thoughts of Mitch. That could wait. The picketing of the Hemstreet businesses now was also of lesser importance when evil had entered her neighborhood. The barrios were hers to protect, hers and her family's responsibility. Whatever had happened, she wanted it solved.

She went back into the house and clicked on Torre's cell.

"Why are you up so early?" her sleepy sister asked.

"Why aren't you?"

"I am on vacation."

"Not any longer. I need you to do some computer work while I follow a hunch."

"Hunch huh?" Her sister sounded more awake. "So what am I doing?"

"Hitting the computer for all of Deborah or Debbie Johnson's social media contacts. Get a list of the names most frequently commenting, sharing or liking, possible boyfriends, and see if you can find any threats."

"Will do. Where is your hunch taking you?"

"I want to see where the body was found, photos if possible, and talk to whoever found her." She had one more plan, but that would depend on what she could sense if the body was where the murder had taken place. They weren't always. She would know the likelihood of that based on physical evidence as well as her own skills.

"All right. Be careful."

"You too. Once you do searches, some may be looking for who you are."

Torre laughed. "If I wasn't a born hacker, I'd be worried. Talk to you later, sis."

An hour later, Elke walked out of the police station having seen the upsetting photos. Jace had agreed to let her follow him out to the crime site. Even though they had found clothing near the body, He had told her they were in doubt whether she had been killed there, based on lack of disturbance and no bodily fluids.

Driving out toward A Mountain, Elke didn't like knowing Nick and Denali were investing in property out that way. Still, there was nothing to connect Nick to the murder. Hopefully, nothing would have been planted to change that.

Jace turned off the main road, down a gravel road, and stopped where police vehicles were parked. "A man hiking with his dog came across the body," Jace said while she changed into tennis shoes to walk down the sandy wash. Its walls were rocky with clay and rubble strewn walls. Saguaros towered above with prickly pear in rocky clefts. They were heavy with their fruit slowly ripening.

"In this heat, that was fortunate." A deteriorating body would quickly lose any chance for an autopsy to reveal anything.

"I think whoever killed her expected it as this is a popular walk in this neighborhood."

"So, you believe the killer wanted her found?"

"You saw the photos of how she was left."

"Yes, intended to look like the others."

"You have reason to believe it wasn't the same killer?" He had gone beyond her words to what intended could mean.

"It happens. If the killer, despite the papers trying to tamp down panic, knew how the first two had been left, this could have multiple reasons for happening."

"I suppose." He didn't sound convinced."

"The first murders were close together. This has been two months."

"Maybe the killer was busy with something else."

She knew what he meant—like a wedding. She said nothing. There was no way to tell Jace who the first murderer had been. She needed evidence that proved this was not the same person. The way the body had been left was one difference. Yes, it was crucifixion posed but naked was different, the bruises were different. The first two killings had been clean, quickly done. The photos she saw of Debbie did not look as though she'd had such a merciful end.

There was yellow tape around the small bluff where the body had been left. With human and animal tracks, no way to know which had anything to do with the murder. At least not for those without extrasensory perception.

She stood, letting the events of the night come to her. She saw a man walking up the draw, his feet sinking into the sand. He was a heavy man who had been carrying a heavy load. He heaved for breath. Not used to such work. Maybe drunk but she couldn't determine that.

She closed her eyes and saw the images of him putting the body against the clay bluff, propping her hands out. She felt no remorse emanating from him, as he worked to position the body and then take her clothing from a backpack. He was wearing rubber gloves. He would leave no trace other than that of energy. No evidence sufficient for a court in that.

"We do not think she was killed here," Jace said repeating what he had earlier said and interrupting her remote viewing of what had happened under the cover of darkness.

The clothing had been left even though the body had been removed. She looked at the little pile. "Have you checked her home to see if that might be where she was killed?" she asked. "She must have gone there after leaving the theater as this isn't what she wore when I saw her."

"We sent forensics there." Jace let out a breath. "I suppose Beringer has an alibi."

She smiled. "You know this wasn't the same man. You have two if not three killers."

"I don't think it was Beringer for any of them, but it's likely he'll be questioned."

"Look for bruised hands then."

"Unless the person wore gloves."

She shrugged. Remote viewing, especially of something that had happened hours earlier, would hardly qualify as evidence. The large overweight man had not been Chuck Carter. Something in her impressions told her the man carrying the body might not have been her murderer. While she had been unable to make out his features, she had felt his energy so strongly that if she met him, she'd know. Once she knew who the man had been, a motive would be easier to track down.

Driving back to town, Elke decided there were two places to start. First would be the ex-con street preacher. There was no logical reason to connect the murder to her family but she felt it intuitively. Whether connected or not, a religious group was stirring up fear and hatred against witches. A starting place should be those who operated in the barrios.

John Donovan worked out of what had been a storefront, south of Barrio Viejo. When she pulled her car over, she saw several men loitering in the shade of the awning. She sent out a wave to detect if any demonic activity was near. She felt nothing and got out of the car.

"I am looking for Reverend Donovan," she asked a surprisingly clean looking guy, who was sitting on the sidewalk. He moved his gaze up to study her. With a t-shirt and jeans, he did not appear like the homeless she'd seen elsewhere. Maybe he worked for the reverend.

"Why?"

"Do I need a reason?"

A laugh came from the building and a big man came out. "Beautiful women never need reasons." He was tall, muscular, without an ounce of fat. She guessed him to be in his early 50s although if he'd led a hard life, that was hard to gauge.

"You are Reverend Donovan?" she asked sure he had to be as she held out her hand, which he took. His grip was firm, his palms rough.

"Call me John."

"I am Elke Hemstreet."

He let out a whistle. "Is Maria a relative?"

She nodded and smiled. "My mother. I hope that is in my favor."

"Of course. Come on in. I have some iced tea if you'd like it."

"I would like."

He had a small room in the back where a cot, one burner stove and small refrigerator told her it was where he lived. The table had mismatched chairs, but everything was clean. It was also blazing hot as the only cooling was a fan overhead to move the air but do nothing for its temperature.

"What can I do for you, Miss Hemstreet?" he asked as he sat across the table from her.

"I wanted to meet you. I had heard about your work. I know your sister-in-law from her paintings."

He grinned. "The beautiful Rachel, yes. She does wonderful work. You haven't met her though?"

"No, but I think some of my family has."

"I was separated from my brother, Jake, for years, blamed him for what I had done. Fortunately, we are now restored. The prodigal son and all that."

"That's wonderful. I know how important family is." She tried to think how to broach what she most wanted to know. It seemed only directly would do. "Are you aware of a movement in Tucson who is trying to drive witches out of their businesses. Of course, we all know witches don't exist." She smiled. "Despite that, it's been my family where the effort has been directed."

"Now, how could anyone think that about such a nice family?"

There was something about the gleam in his eyes, which turned his comment ironic.

"I didn't realize ministers could have a sense of humor," she retorted.

He laughed. "Can they?"

"Some it appears."

"I am teasing you. I am also maybe not the usual preacher. I value spirituality in whatever form it comes and see those who do good may come from many walks and ways." He smiled again.

"I had heard there were two pastors working in this neighborhood. You are, of course, one."

"And Martin Jefferies is the other with Faith in Action."

"That is the name I heard. I suppose pastors never speak ill of each other."

Again, that gleam. "Loyalty to the brand."

"Of course."

"Since I am not your traditional preacher, I don't have that. I have met Pastor Jefferies. He does not think much of my ministry nor do I of his."

"I plan to meet him next."

"Don't expect it will change his mind when you do. Some people need an enemy. Witches are good for that purpose—especially after the Potter books attempted to make it more acceptable and now, of course, *Vislogus*."

"You read it?" She was surprised.

"I read them both."

"Well, it may not help to talk to him, but I do want to try." She didn't mention her other reason—the murder of Debbie Johnson. Her reasons for thinking there might be a connection were nothing she could discuss with this minister.

"Of course, one can always try." He smiled again. She liked him and was glad her mother had been involved in furthering his ministry. It seemed a positive element for the barrios. His energy was not that of the man who had placed the body in the wash.

Before heading for Faith in Action, she called Torre's cell. "Find anything useful?" she asked.

"Debbie went to University of Arizona but dropped out her

freshman year. She'd been working at a local church as a secretary for two years."

"Faith in Action."

"Yep. She also has been very involved on several social media sites, hundreds of friends if having names there means friends. There were the usual interests of young women as to hot men and sexy clothes, good shoes, many hopes for the future when she'd be a big star. From her photos, she was pretty, which you knew. Unfortunately, for her dreams, besides being murdered, there are many pretty women out there. She was trying to get parts in other theater productions but had only been a secondary player."

"Was she a member of the congregation where she worked?"

"She didn't list it, if so. Most of her likes were rather innocuous, the sort you do because everybody else does, if you know what I mean."

"Okay, thanks. I am heading to that church next."

"You sure you know what you're doing?"

"Maybe." Elke laughed. "And look up Chuck Carter. Or Charles. See what you come up with—especially if he ends up on Debbie's friend list."

"Okay."

"I met John Donovan just now. He seems nice. I guess Mom donates to his work." She knew Torre was more into the Hemstreet charitable work than she had been.

"That and two others who help the homeless."

"Okay, if you don't hear from me by seven tonight, come get me because I will not be willingly converting." She laughed with Torre but wasn't sure it was actually funny.

She had considered getting an appointment to speak with Pastor Jefferies but opted instead for surprise. She wanted to get a sense of his energy when he was not expecting her. She had seen the outside of the church but hadn't thought much of it other than it was a large building with few ornamentations. Where she saw two cars parked, she decided was most likely the office. Again, she felt for energies. This time she was blocked. Something was around or that would not happen.

Getting out of her car, the heat was like a blast that threatened to cook everything in its path. It felt even hotter than south of town? The pavement looked melted. The door opened at her light touch. She began to feel uneasy about her plan. There was no turning back.

"May I help you?" An older woman was behind a desk. Her hair was cut short. She wore no makeup. The long-sleeved, green dress completed a Spartan look. Air-conditioning, running hard, kept the room at maybe 70°. It was a bit of a shock to her system.

"Would Reverend Jefferies be available today?"

The woman studied her. "May I say the purpose for which you are asking?"

"I knew Debbie Johnson."

The woman's face twisted. "The police were here… It was so tragic. Just a moment, let me see if he is able to speak to you." She punched a number. "There is a young lady here to speak to you about Debbie." She nodded. "You may go in." She pointed to the door behind her.

After the very plain reception room, the pastor's office came as a shock. It was painted a vibrant burgundy with a plush sofa and two stuffed chairs as well as a large ebony desk. A bookcase behind the desk was full of books with matching covers. The air was warmer than the outside office but still pleasantly cool. This church didn't mind spending money on more than protests.

"You were a friend of Debbie's?" he asked as he extended his hand. She took it, finding it strange that she got no information regarding his energy.

"More an acquaintance. I saw her last night at the theater."

"Theater?"

"Stage Left. She was there along with your brother, David, and several other actors as we discussed a possible play for the fall."

"And your name is?"

"Elke Hemstreet."

"I see. Are you the owner of the shop and the bookstore?"

"My family."

"So it's not about Deborah that you came." His smile was close to a sneer.

"It was, as I knew she worked for you."

"Yes, she had."

"Had?"

"She had quit the day before. We hadn't even run the papers through. I told the police all of this. I feel very badly for her, but it seemed she was heading a way that this was the likely end. Her desire for theater… well, you can see the conflict."

"Theater is evil?"

"Some of them."

"Your brother's?"

"It wasn't just that. Women who dress to provoke often find the result is someone being provoked."

"Debbie wasn't wearing anything that provocative when I saw her at the theater. She was dressed like many young girls."

"I am afraid I cannot help you. You and I are on separate paths." There was something in his eyes that let her know a warning had been given. "Short skirts like yours, bare arms, flowing hair, well, it does lead to trouble. I hope you will see that—before it's too late."

"Is that why you believe my sister and I are witches?"

"Oh no, that came as the result of hours of prayer."

She tried but could not resist. "Prayer to whom?" He looked blankly at her, as she rose. "I am sorry to have bothered you."

"Sorry I could not help you," he said as he walked her to the door.

"I did have one more question."

"Of course." His smile was repugnant.

"Is Chuck or Charles Carter a member of your congregation?" she asked before she went into the searing heat.

"Never heard the name. Good luck, my dear." His expression gave away nothing.

As she got into her car, Elke knew her family had an enemy, a directed and dangerous one. Although she'd never seen the face in her vision of the man carrying Debbie's body, Jefferies fit the body type, but something in that office had blocked her ability to read his energy. None of which proved anything. Neither did the way he had looked at her. She would have to double the wards around her home from now on—at least until they found Debbie's murderer.

"Hell," Mitch growled as he shoved the last bag into the bed of the truck. He had planned to leave with dark. He put the hitch onto the back of the truck feeling even more angry and frustrated. His horse trailer was at the ranch where he would get Ranger before heading north. His mind was on none of that.

"What's wrong?" Adolph asked, letting the rabbit go, that he had only been half-heartedly chasing.

It was too hot. Maybe that was all Mitch was feeling. Except he knew it wasn't. "It's that woman," he said finally as he straightened and stared toward the city.

Adolph gave a wolf smile. "The beautiful one?"

"You know which one." Mitch was disgusted and angry at himself. He couldn't let it go. She was in trouble—more than she knew. It wasn't his problem. She wasn't his problem. Ever since he'd read the morning paper, seen a third woman had been killed, he'd had a bad feeling. Throughout the day, as he'd readied the house to be left, his premonition had grown.

He could feel energies building-- ugly and dark, threatening. He needed to leave Tucson, to go north where he could think more clearly and better protect himself. He had sent Buck and Sofia ahead to ready the house. It was time for him to go. Elke Hemstreet wasn't in danger.

Except he knew she was. The dark elements were growing. She had already made herself a target. She didn't have a clue what she would soon face. Swearing under his breath, he told Adolph, "Get in the truck."

"You aren't in a good mood. Don't do something with that woman that you'll regret."

"I won't." He headed down the driveway pushing the remote to close the gate behind him. He hoped his home would be there when he returned.

"How do you know where to find her?" Adolph asked, when he turned south not north when he reached the main road. In the distance, a thick lightning bolt slammed into Wasson Peak.

"I know." That made him mad too, that he did know. That ever since she had come to his home he had wanted to know more about her, about what she did, where she lived. He knew and knowing infuriated him.

Driving across Tucson, the storm seemed to be staying in the Tucson Mountains, as it slammed again and again to one or the other of the peaks. Overhead it was a clear sky filled with stars while the opposite mountains were being hammered. The blackness above was enhanced by no moonlight. Its sliver wouldn't rise until 3 am.

Beyond downtown Tucson, he turned into the old barrio. He didn't need to read the street signs. He knew where she was by scent. He stopped the truck in front of a two story, older home. She would be in the upper level. There were no lights on. Fine, he had no intention of knocking. "Stay with the truck," he told Adolph as he got out. A figure walked out of the shadows and headed toward the gated entrance. At the metal grill, the male pulled a knife and began to jimmy the lock.

Mitch smiled. "Looking for something?" he asked quietly, as he walked up behind the man, who turned with the knife in his hand. Mitch reached out and grabbed his wrist, twisting it hard enough to force him to drop the knife before he heard the bone snap over his knee. The man let out a yelp of pain. "Worse happens if you don't get out of here," Mitch warned. The man grasped his broken arm, wheeled, and sprinted out of sight. Mitch kicked the knife into the oleander.

Directing his powers toward the lock, he heard it click open and walked through. At the top of the stairs, there was a door. Again, the lock was no problem, and he walked into the silent apartment. Small kitchen to the left, living room in front of him and a door down a short hall that had to be to the bedroom. He stalked toward it angry and ready to tear something apart that he was even doing this.

As he opened the door, a flare of energy shot toward him, which he blocked with his hand, throwing it to the ground. "Now was that nice?" he asked realizing that she wasn't quite as defenseless as he had assumed.

"Neither is breaking into someone's home," she snapped. She was sitting in the center of her bed wearing a filmy gown. Without light, he saw only the shadowy shape and thought that was a good thing as what he was thinking now took his anger to a different level.

"You're coming with me," he said.

"Why would I do that?"

"Because you aren't safe here. Did you know someone was breaking in when I got here?"

"I had heard the sound and was ready."

"For anything?"

She gave a little laugh. "Apparently not."

"Get dressed, grab some clothes, and hurry up."

"I am going nowhere with you."

"You have a choice of packing some clothes and walking out of here, or you can be carried with just what you are wearing. That's your only choice."

She glared at him. "To where?"

"Verde Valley and my ranch there. There is a problem here in Tucson. I want to be where I can figure out what is happening and maybe why."

"And that will be easier when not here? Seems it'd be the other way around."

"Lady, I'm done arguing." He headed for her.

"Wait. I'll get dressed. Turn around."

"Why? So you can throw another plasma bolt at me?" he asked.

"I didn't know it was you when I threw it." She got off the bed, and he turned around, heard the rustle of clothing as the fabric dropped, and then she was pulling on clothing. "I think I'd be safe here. My family is here."

"For now they aren't the target. Do you want to change that?"

"Good point."

"Make sure you include jeans and if you have them boots."

He heard her opening drawers and throwing clothing into what was probably a bag. He concentrated on what was outside. Adolph would warn him if another came, but he wanted out of this neighborhood, away from Tucson where he could think clearly. That is if clear thinking was ever going to be possible around her. What he was doing made no sense but then that wasn't new.

CHAPTER 7

S itting in the truck alongside Mitch, with Adolph moved to the back seat, Elke found it difficult to comprehend how abruptly things had changed. She was with the man she wanted to be with but not as she had imagined. She had realized someone was trying to open the lower gate but never imagined it was Mitch.

"It wasn't me," he said as he turned east, away from town.

"You read minds?"

"When needed, but in this case, you logically might've wondered. I don't know who it was, but he has a broken arm now."

She wasn't surprised. Mitch was a powerful and even deadly looking man, especially when he was in the mood to be. "Recently," she said, "you didn't even want to talk to me. What changed?"

"I'll tell you later if that's okay."

"All right, but at least, where are we going? This isn't heading north."

"I have to pick up Ranger. I think your foreman has gone as far as he can with him."

She settled back trying to decide how she felt about any of what had just happened. "I knew you had a horse there but didn't know why. Luke wouldn't help me find your address."

"He's a good man." She saw a faint smile but wasn't sure it was genuine. He was clearly troubled. Coming to her, as he had, showed the caliber of the man, where he would put someone else's needs

72

ahead of his own. She supposed she could use that knowledge to try and convince him to let her use his book. Even the thought felt unethical. Maybe she could find another book that would accomplish the same purposes—not as good, of course.

"He is skilled with horses," she said as they turned onto the road to the ranch. Behind them, the storm was moving up the valley but strangely had left the east side mostly alone.

"Ranger is jittery. He doesn't like wolves." He gave a little laugh.

"And you like to ride with Adolph."

"It is one problem." She knew there was more but again, she could wait. She was going with him wherever that was. She'd let him think he was forcing her. She could have put an end to that if she had wanted- she didn't want. Suddenly, she very much wanted wherever they were heading.

"I need to let my mother know where I am. The family will go nuts without my telling them."

"They won't just know?" It wasn't much of a question.

She considered that. Since she had not been in danger, her mother might not have recognized what was happening. "I guess they would eventually but why worry them."

"Do you text?"

"As little as possible. Mom isn't good with electronic devices of any sort."

"Hmmm." He turned into the drive that led to the hacienda and barns.

"Will Luke be expecting you?"

"Originally I planned to take Ranger for a ride. He was to have him in the main stable. I can leave him a note, and he can let your mother know. I think that might be best."

"You really think I am targeted?"

"In two ways."

He wasn't much for lengthy answers. She herself had come to believe the demonstrations and murder were connected. What was his source to add her to the mix? He pulled in front of the barn, backed up to a trailer and turned to look at her as he unfastened his seat belt. "I won't be long."

"Do you need help with hitching the trailer or getting your horse in?"

"Nope. How about you write a note to Luke for both of us." He reached under his seat for a pad and pen. "He'll know to be careful how he gets it to Maria."

Watching him in the mirrors as he smoothly attached the trailer to the truck, she knew she was with Adolfo. He wasn't fictional. Adolfo had been a warrior who could overpower the strongest of monsters. Perhaps Mitch had fudged some on the abilities. When he disappeared into the barn, she looked at his wolf in the mirror. "How about it, Adolph? Is he all Adolfo Lupan is?" She wasn't really expecting an answer.

"And more," the wolf said.

She turned in her seat and met the wolf's level gaze. "You aren't all you seem either."

"Are you?" The wolf gave one of those smiles, that in her experience, only wolves could manage.

"Is anybody?" She heard hooves and watched as Mitch easily led his horse into the trailer. Then she remembered her assignment and quickly wrote a note explaining going north with Ranger. And asked Luke to let her mother know she would be along—but keep it quiet. She'd let more explanations wait for when she better understood herself.

When he got back to the truck, he grabbed a wipe to clean his hands, then took her note and put it in the barn.

Once he was driving again, she said, "So what will we talk about going north?" She glanced at him with a grin.

"You like conversation on the road," he said without enthusiasm.

"How about talk radio then? There is a late night alternative reality talk show." She laughed when he made a face. "Music?"

"What kind do you like?"

"Everything old. Barry Manilow is right up my alley."

She was teasing and got the expected response. "Maybe we can talk," he said. "The cold box is right behind you if you want a drink."

"What would you like?" She opened the lid and saw cans of iced tea, Coke, lemonade, 7-Up, and bottled water. On the floor was a bowl with water for Adolph.

He turned onto the main road leading to the freeway. "Nothing for now."

"You haven't been very talkative."

"I can be. Offer a topic."

"Adolph."

"Go ahead."

"Your wolf thinks highly of you."

"And you know this why?" He glanced over at her.

"He told me so."

"He doesn't talk to just anyone, so who is Elke Hemstreet, that he'd trust you?"

"You already know, just as I know you are Adolfo Lupan, even if maybe with less of his skills or maybe not."

"So the demonstrators were right."

"Not about who witches are."

"Witch though you may be, you are not superhuman, are you?"

She shook her head. "No, and I already know you can bleed. What I don't know is who you are."

"Are you hungry?" he asked, avoiding answering.

"You have food along also?"

"Sure, the other cold box. I would have to stop to open that one. Sandwiches, cut up fruit, vegetables, cold cuts for Adolph." He smiled for the first time with warmth. Turning onto the freeway, he asked, "Did you know who was trying to visit you?"

"I could only guess. There is a man who has been irritating me with unwanted attentions. There is another possibility though. Today, I visited Pastor Jefferies."

"Bill's brother?"

"He runs a church that is opposed to the occult."

"Not too unusual in religions—especially where it comes to witches." His smile was again actually amused. "At one time, that meant burning at the stake or hanging."

"I think he's not going quite that far." She smiled too. "Despite his aggressive approach encouraging his parishioners, I don't believe he'd send someone to break into my home."

"Maybe to scare you."

"I suppose."

"You were investigating the most recent murder, weren't you?"

"I was looking into it. Not that we had been hired, but I had met the victim earlier the night she was murdered. She had been at the meeting when we discussed the fall production. Do you know David Jefferies?"

"Just by name."

"He had invited a few actors as well as Pamela Crosby who does makeup and I think is David's current lady love." She smiled. "I can't believe that was all just Monday evening. My world seems to have been cramming a lot into a few short hours."

"You talked to them about using my book?"

"I did. I looked back at that meeting for any clue I should have had that Debbie was in danger. There was nothing. I learned after her murder that she worked as a secretary for Martin Jefferies at his church, Faith in Action."

"Is she why you went there?"

"I thought the protests and the murder might be connected. I also visited John Donovan."

"Now, him I know. He runs the street church south of Tucson."

"And you donated to his work."

"He makes a difference."

"He seems very authentic."

"So, in your research, did you look me up before you came to ask me about using my book?"

"I admit I tried. There was virtually nothing online about you. I suppose that was purposeful."

"You could have used other methods, given who your family is." He glanced over at her before changing lanes to pass a semi.

"I suppose, but I didn't. My family has strict rules about how magick can be used."

He nodded. "Do you know who Robert Flynn was?"

"Of course, everybody does, don't they? I loved his films on the movie channels and used to rent them as DVDs." She suddenly saw the resemblance. "He was your father, wasn't he?"

"Something I only learned when my grandfather was dying. I am a half-breed, Miss Hemstreet. My mother was pure Apache. She died at my birth. My father never knew of my existence until I showed up at his door."

"Did he take it well?"

"After he got over the shock. He couldn't really deny it."

"I realize now how much you resemble him."

"I don't talk about it, don't tell people until I get to know them better. It's not that I'm ashamed of it, but I didn't want to succeed because of who he was."

"I am trying to understand then from where the book came. Surely not him?"

He smiled again. "No, that would be my great grandfather, and I guess inherited abilities."

"You were fortunate to know your great grandfather."

She saw him hesitate. "He came to me from the other side, Miss Hemstreet."

"Elke."

"He came to me as a guide, Elke. He had died before I was born."

"Apache mysticism."

"You aren't sounding surprised by that, even if you were about Robert Flynn."

"I know a bit about shamans. My family claims Yaqui ancestry." They had more in common than she had imagined.

When they approached Phoenix, she looked over at his profile, intent now on the highway. He handled the truck well, especially considering the horse trailer on behind. He had secure the gelding well, as the trailer wasn't shifting the truck. Adolph had seemed to be enjoying the drive as he watched with enthusiasm out the window. Mitch lowered the rear window a bit for the wolf to scent the air. Once they got through Phoenix traffic, lighter as it was for being nearly three, she saw the glow to the east. "The moon is coming up," she said.

"Right on time."

"A new moon. A good time for planting."

"You follow astrology?"

"Don't you?"

"What do you think a new moon is good for?"

She had to think about whether she wanted to tell him. "It's for starting over, new beginnings." She didn't add also for love and romance. She didn't want to kick her own imagination into overdrive. She paid more attention to the moon cycles than maybe she should.

"The new moon is a time for wishes," he said, "for thinking what you want to make manifest. From now until the full moon is a good time for prophecy, protection, divination." When she looked over at him, he winked before turning his attention back to the highway. "Maybe I know a little about it."

"Maybe you do." She smiled then and leaned back against the seat. She liked riding with him. His handling of the truck was smooth, as he wove through what traffic there was and then headed beyond Black Canyon for the climb toward the Verde Valley.

"So, what do you want to make manifest in your life?" he asked as he set the truck on cruise control with the traffic thinning to only a few long-distance travelers.

"Would it be safe for me to tell you?" she asked putting a deliberately teasing note to her voice.

"Of course, I wrote *Vislogus*. You know all about my good intentions."

She laughed at his pious tone. "There were no love scenes in it. Maybe your good intentions change when testosterone enters the picture."

"Ah but I am a monk. Dedicated to spiritual pursuits." She looked over to see the expression on his face, but a fast moving police car raced by. Mitch's only expression was directed to the highway.

"And that's why Adolph's friend, Estella, got nowhere in attracting his interest as she wanted," she suggested when the road was again theirs.

He glanced over at her. "You were disappointed it didn't have a romance?" He laughed.

"Of course. Isn't that what everyone wants?"

"Romances usually end badly."

"You mean love stories. Romances must have a happily ever after."

"Not very realistic."

"Of course not, that's what newspapers are for."

He chuckled. "So you read romances and imagine happy endings, but then don't you find life disappointing?"

"I guess so... sometimes. My sister seems to have found her happily ever after."

"How long have they been married?"

"Not quite two months."

"Get back to me in two years."

"You are a cynic."

"And you didn't recognize that in *Vislogus*?"

"Actually, I didn't. I thought Adolfo was a true believer in the power of good to win out."

"In some situations. The emotion we call love is not one of them."

"Is your disillusionment about love something you discovered in your own life?"

"That's a rather snoopy question."

"For a man who kidnapped me, I think it's a fair one."

"I did not kidnap you."

"Did you give me a choice?"

"Two of them." She glanced over and saw the smile.

"I'll let that go for now. I would have resisted more had I not wanted to come."

"And I'll let you believe that might've changed things."

This time she smiled. "I have more powers than a plasma bolt."

"Good. I will worry less about you… if I believed it anyway."

"What do you know about witches?"

"Very little." He glanced over at her. "I expect I will learn more though."

"She talks to animals," Adolph offered from the backseat.

"All animals?" Mitch asked. "Or just the ones who aren't exactly the expected?"

"If they can communicate and hear, I can talk to them," she said. "Did you try that with Ranger?"

"There is a little problem there. He doesn't trust me. I am hoping Luke will have changed that."

Suddenly she knew why. "You are a wolf shifter." It was another thing they had in common, but she wasn't going to tell him that yet. It might come in handy at some future point for him to end up surprised.

He didn't admit it. "I want to ride with Adolph."

She had never had a problem with horses distrusting her despite her own enjoyment of occasionally shifting into a wolf. "Maybe you are too aggressive with Ranger," she suggested.

"I can ride my other horses."

"How many do you have?"

"Fiona and Pepper, mares. Traveler, another gelding, and Major, my stallion. None of them have been so flighty as Ranger. I saw it as something about wolves."

"I will try talking to him when we get there," she said smiling as he gave her one of his looks.

"And you will have better luck than I've had or for that matter Adolph?"

"Does Ranger talk to you?"

"No."

"So let me try."

"Sure, give it a shot."

"And when we get there, do we try to figure out what's going on in Tucson, so I can go home."

"How about we take a day to unwind. You might like my ranch."

"I expect to but people are being killed in Tucson, and I worry that someone is trying to set up my brother-in-law as the murderer."

"And you know he's not."

"Yes."

"Not just because your sister married him?"

"No."

"All right." He turned off the freeway onto the exit for the Verde Valley. Even in the dim light of early dawn, she liked what she saw. She'd spent more time in Sedona than this part of the Verde, but there was a natural and laidback feeling to this country. The river wound below the highway, visible only now and then. This land still had the feel of the Sinagua who had lived here before the first Apaches and then Euromericans appeared. Because of the rich river bottom, it had long been valued and fought over.

"How long have you owned your ranch?" she asked.

"It was my father's—same with the Tucson house. He used this one as a personal retreat, a place to escape. He loved it and took me here as soon as he and I met. We had a chance to talk, to ride. I feel him here always. His ashes are spread in a special place he had requested."

"It's wonderful to have a place with that deep of meaning."

"The Circle C is not that for you?"

"Not really. It's my mother's of course. I go out there, and we have a place we meet as a family. I don't consider it mine." She realized she had no place that she felt that way about. "I do love Barrio Viejo, have worked with others to see the neighborhood stays as it is, but it's not really mine either."

He drove past Cottonwood and then Clarksdale. She began to wonder exactly where his land might be and then he turned north on a small road, all but invisible until on it. "Is your winery out here?" she asked.

"Yes, the vineyard anyway and the building where Jacques makes and ages the wine. The shop and tasting room are in Cotton-wood—well, between it and Clarksdale. The vineyard is open once a year, by invitation only, when the new wines are introduced." The road wound into the hills above the Verde and dimly she saw the dark cut of another canyon. "What is out there?" she asked pointing to it.

"Sycamore Canyon. We overlook it and the Verde." He crossed a small bridge, obviously a private one. She'd seen no gate. "Aren't you bothered by trespassers?" she asked thinking of the big gate on his Tucson estate.

"Rarely. The ones who know it's here, connoisseurs of fine wines, aren't that impressed by authors or movie stars. My land stretches to the Mogollon Plateau. I've bought more as the opportunity has arisen. Beyond it is national forest."

"How did you know it would do so well on growing grapes?"

"Research, once I knew I wanted to do this. It's similar in soils and elevation to parts of Lebanon and Iran where they first made wine. Grapes get a richness when they have to struggle a little to survive. Maybe not so many to harvest but more flavorful. This has been volcanic, had floods, layers of minerals."

He made another turn and then she saw the house. It was two stories, with a deck on the second floor that ran its length. Red tile roof, chimneys for fireplaces. It was simpler than the estate in Tucson, looked to have been here a long time, and had a hominess, to which she was immediately drawn.

"It's not as big as Tucson, but this is where I can think."

"Where you wrote *Vislogus*, I guess."

"It was." He pulled around behind, and she saw the stables and corrals. When he stopped the truck, he got out and opened the door for Adolph. She walked to the corrals, while he opened up the trailer to back Ranger come out. "Hey boy," he said, "you're home. Like it better now?"

The gelding whinnied, and she heard an answer from the corrals as the other horses galloped to greet the arrival. Another whinny came from a corral above the stable. She guessed that to be the stallion as he galloped to the fence in an aggressive mode.

"Major thinks he runs things here," Mitch said as he led Ranger to the lower corrals and let him in before removing his halter. "Pretty much he does."

"Your stallion isn't bothered by the wolf scent?" she asked watching as the horses greeted each other like old friends.

"Maybe he was one in a previous life," Mitch said as he walked back to her.

"You believe in transmigration?"

"Among other things."

"And those would be?"

"Getting some sleep. Do you want to eat first?"

"No."

"Okay, then I'll show you your room." He picked up her bag. "Buck and Sofia arrived earlier. I have a stable guy, but he lives off the ranch."

Inside the house, she saw natural wood, a feeling of a mountain cabin but larger, as the room soared to a second level. Navajo rugs and even animal skulls were on the walls. She followed him up a set of open stairs to a balcony. "Bedrooms at each end," he said. "You can have your pick of three. Buck and Sofia are on the main floor. Mine is at the other end of the balcony. You won't be bothered here."

In the first room, she liked its opening onto the veranda. "This will be fine."

"We can talk tomorrow after you wake up." He set her bag on the dresser. "The kitchen is to the back when you come down." With that, he was gone, and she was left to wonder what kind of rabbit hole she'd fallen down.

She felt tempted to call her mother, but he was right. She didn't know who was behind the murder of Debbie or whether Pastor Jefferies had some kind of demonic power behind him. She would bet any power he had was not coming from the Light.

To add to the questions, she also didn't know who had tried to enter her home, when Mitch stopped him. She should have tried harder to figure that out at the time, but she'd only sensed the invasion and waited to deal with it. It could have been Chuck Clark but equally could have been someone from Action in Faith.

Feeling suddenly exhausted, she stripped and got under the sheets. She spent a few moments to set up a ward around the house as she didn't have the feeling there was one—not that her earlier ward had kept out Mitch. In the morning, when she woke, it would all be clearer. Then she realized it was morning. It would all be clearer when she woke.

CHAPTER 8

Mitch let himself sleep a couple of hours but had too much to do to take more. In the kitchen, Sofia had prepared coffee. "What would you like?" she asked. "I have eggs, bread, ham, bacon, orange juice, potatoes."

He grinned and poured his coffee. "Surprise me." He opened a can of food for Adolph and walked to the kitchen window to look over his land. Never had he been to the Verde ranch when he hadn't felt peace descending over him. Even now, with turmoil threatening, having brought a reluctant woman with him, even then, he knew this was where he needed to be—the land of his Apache ancestors and his father.

When Robert Flynn bought the ranch, he told Mitch later that he'd called it the Flying Flynn as a kind of joke since he'd done a fair number of action thrillers including pirate movies. Now, while Mitch called the vineyard Vislogus, this ranch was in all the important ways —a place with no name. It owned him as much as he owned it.

Maybe finally here, Nantan Lupan would return, get over being angry with him, and provide him guidance again. He had waited, hoping, asking, but he understood the old man's annoyance when he felt Mitch had let him down.

"Good morning," Elke said from the door. Adolph left his food to greet her before he went back to eating.

"I didn't know he brought you, missy. What can I get you?" Sofia smiled and gestured for Elke to sit while she brought her coffee.

"What are my options?" Elke asked. When Sofia listed them off, Elke said, "Surprise me."

Mitch came to sit across the table from her. "I thought you'd sleep longer."

She sipped her coffee. "My mind wouldn't let me."

"I'm sorry I insisted you come. I was reacting to an urge I can't explain right now. I can take you back if you wish."

"No, I've thought about it. Your urge was right. I didn't know what was happening. I was trying to sort it out but kept going in circles. Maybe we'll have better luck together."

"You need cream or sugar for your coffee?" Sofia asked as she refilled Mitch's cup.

"Black, thank you." She looked at him. "I can understand why you wanted to come here. It's beautiful with a wonderful feel to it."

"After we eat, would you like to go for a ride? I can show you the whole place from horseback."

"I'd love it."

An hour later, he saddled Pepper for her and Ranger for himself. The gelding danced a little when Adolph approached, but settled down and didn't fight the bridle or being saddled. If he'd been more confident in the horse's temperament, he'd have used a hackamore. For now, the bit was going in. He watched as Elke mounted before he swung into his own saddle.

"I've never been in this part of the Verde Valley," she said as he headed them north and to a trail he'd taken often that would bring them onto a ridge where they'd see the vineyard and the valley laid out as well as the distant Sycamore creek. Adolph raced ahead scenting out rabbits and whatever varmints had been there, since the last rain.

"I suppose you were in Sedona for the woo-woo events," he teased.

"You mean vortex ceremonies. No, we have a vortex on the Circle C. They can be found many places. I've been for Tlaquepaque, the resorts, swimming, the art galleries."

"Your family was a fan of the arts before Beringer entered it?"

"My mother and maybe some my father. None of their daughters though inherited that particular talent. The closest is Denali who paints, what I consider good work, but she never thought it was. I can't draw a straight line." She laughed.

"You recognize it though as you do pick out clothing that will appeal."

"Ah yes, Mellow Yellow. That only takes seeing what others have created and convincing someone else it will make them beautiful." She looked over at him. "Have you been to the shop?"

He shook his head. "I looked you up after you left. Only fair, don't you think?" He tightened his rein on Ranger as he felt him try to turn back. "Maybe he's just got a stubborn streak," he said as the gelding responded to his steady hand.

"Is this a good place to let them go?" she asked. "Maybe he needs to run it out."

He smiled. "Excellent place. Head for the red rock ridge you see at the top of this trail." With that, he nudged Ranger in the side, and the two horses took off at a gallop. He stayed a little back enjoying watching how smoothly Elke rode. At the excitement of the running horses, Adolph returned but kept enough distance from Ranger not to frighten him.

At the bluff, Elke pulled Pepper to a halt. She looked at the rocks. "Petroglyphs."

"There are a lot of them around here. Five other sites on this ranch."

"Do you know what they mean?"

"Not the Sinagua petroglyphs, but the pictograph shield to the left is Apache. It's establishment of territory. This was Apache land after the old ones left. Some say the zigzag marks are clans, but I don't know anybody who can say for sure."

He turned his horse and pointed out the vineyards now far below. "My father ran cattle on here, but I haven't done that. I am not here enough. If they got into the vineyard, Jacques would likely slit my throat." He laughed.

"What kinds of grapes do you raise? I will tell you though, before you start, I know little about wine. My sister,Torre, is the aficionada. She's the one that told me about your winery. According to her, your vintner is world renown."

He nodded. "So I was told when I began this project. I liked the idea though of growing the grapes. Jacques let me know which ones he saw doing well on these slopes. We grow Syrah, Petite Sirah,

Mourvedre, Grenache, and Cabernet Pfeffer grapes. As you said about your being no artist, I am not a vintner. I was lucky that Jacques liked the idea of living in the Verde Valley." Not to mention his ability to reward his skills with a high salary and benefits.

"I can see why you want to be here."

"It gets hot or will this afternoon, but the nights are usually cool. It's quiet here. I can think."

"Are you writing more books?"

"Can we go for the easy questions first?" he asked. "How about whether there is a heaven or hell." He leaned forward on the pommel and grinned.

"Witches aren't on the inside of that."

"You talk to guides, don't you?"

"When needed."

He laughed. "You are as reluctant to talk about yourself as I have been."

"Have?" She laughed.

"I told you about my father. I don't tell many that."

"But there is more, isn't there?"

"Maybe. Let's head back and sample some of that wine."

Adolph came running up and startled Ranger sending him into a bucking frenzy. Not expecting it, Mitch held on for three hard landings, before he was sent sailing, landing hard on his right hand and feeling the pain surge up his arm. "Damn," he cursed, watching Ranger head for the ranch. "I should've shot him." He groaned with the pain. Likely, he'd broken his wrist. Just what he needed.

Watching Mitch be thrown, Elke suppressed her scream. She jumped off her mare, dropped the reins to keep her where she was, and went to where he was levering himself up. "Are you hurt?" Adolph loped to his side and nuzzled him for reassurance.

He snorted. "My pride... and my wrist. Might be a little karma." His laugh was swallowed by a reluctant groan.

She saw then how he was holding his arm. "Let me see what I can do," she said. Healing had been one of her skills, but she'd never tried it on a broken bone. She pushed him flat.

"What are you doing?" he asked, sucking in a breath, as he cursed again.

"Let's see." She put one hand on his wrist, feeling for the energy of the break. Luckily, it wasn't compound. The other hand she held over where she felt the heat of injury. She let the energy of the universe flow through her. The heat grew as waves of it traveled from her, through the air, to his wrist. She moved to hold her other hand over his arm but not touching his skin now. The healing wasn't her. It was the earth, the Elementals, the land that he loved now returning the favor.

She didn't know how long she continued, but eventually she felt a cooling of the skin. The energy changed. "How does it feel?" she asked as she met his gaze for the first time.

"Better." He reached up with his other hand to her neck. He pulled her toward him, not applying enough pressure that she could not have broken away. She didn't want to break way. His lips parted, and she knew hers had too. She wanted the kiss.

The sound of pounding hooves caused him to release her and lever himself up onto his elbow.

"What the hell happened, boss?" the cowboy yelled as he pulled his horse to a plunging stop. He was riding bareback and clearly was at least part Native American.

"I got careless," Mitch said. He rose to his feet and felt of his wrist. "No real damage done though." He looked back at Elke. "Elke, this is Joe Kuruk, my cousin or second cousin or... What the hell relation are we, Joe?" he asked with a laugh.

"Damned if I know."

"Well, the gist of it is when I'm not here, he runs the ranch—the part that Jacques doesn't run at least. Joe, this is Elke Hemstreet."

"Howdy, pretty lady," Joe said. His smile flashed white teeth. He was a handsome man, looked to be tall.

"Pretty and handy to have around too," Mitch said. "Mind if I ride behind you?" he asked as he lifted Elke into her saddle. "Pepper should be fine with the extra weight since it's not far." She leaned forward as he made a leap onto the back of the mare.

"I take it Ranger was fine," Mitch said as they rode down the trail, Adolph running ahead and checking out scents.

"Jittery like before. That horse may not be good for here."

"We'll see."

"Can I try with him?" she asked.

He put his arm around her waist and leaned forward to whisper in her ear. "After you healing my wrist, how could I say no?"

She smiled and leaned against him. "Maybe it wasn't that badly injured."

"You and I both know it was broken. You healed it. Part of the gift of witches?"

"Or shamans." She liked the feel of Mitch's hard body against her. She was beginning to feel urges where it came to him that were new to her. She'd only been with one man sexually and that was in college when it was a *wham bam thank you ma'am,* and she'd decided experimenting with sex wasn't for her. After that, she'd had a few boyfriends but none that lasted long enough for her to consider going beyond brief, goodnight kisses—probably why they hadn't lasted.

"Maybe you want me riding ahead," Joe teased, not catching their conversation but obviously aware of the body language.

"Nah," Mitch said. "I appreciate you riding out to check on me."

Joe chuckled. "Looked like you were doing fine when I rode up, *boss.*"

"Joe thinks being my cousin gives him special privileges," Mitch told her. "Like calling me boss the way he just did."

"You ain't my boss?" Joe asked looking over and winking at Elke.

"No man is your boss, and you don't have a woman yet."

"You got a woman now, *boss?*"

"She's a partner… in crime," Mitch retorted.

"Damn," Joe said. "The world won't be safe."

"Of course it will," Elke said, "just on our terms."

Joe looked over and laughed. "Don't let her get away." Again the wink. "Or tell you what, let her get away, and I'll go round her up."

At the stable, Joe took the horses to rub them down. Elke headed over to the corral where Ranger was looking at them uneasily. She entered the corral and walked toward the gelding. "You are afraid. Tell me why," she said as he pranced a little but waited and let her run her hand over his neck. She stroked him.

'He's a wolf,' the horse told her, 'and he has a wolf who runs with him.'

She smiled at that. She switched to her own thought waves. 'I am also. Did you know that?'

The horse looked at her. 'You don't feel the same.'

'It's because I am female.'

88

She could see Ranger consider that. She continued to stroke him, to use her magick to relax him. 'A wolf killed one of my friends,' Ranger said finally.

'I am sorry to hear that. Wolves are not all the same.' Ranger then looked over at Mitch who, watching them, was leaning his elbows on the top rail of the fence.

'You trust him?' he asked looking back at her.

'I do. You can too. He will protect you. You hurt him today, but he's not angry or punishing you, is he?'

'No.'

'Want me to ride you next time, so you can see I trust him and now you?'

'No, I will not do it again.' The horse then nuzzled her neck. 'You don't feel like a wolf.'

She smiled. 'I will prove it to you someday.' She glanced back at Mitch. 'He doesn't know, so don't tell him yet.'

Ranger snorted and moved from her to Mitch where he let him run his hand down his nose.

"It will be all right now," she said as she came to stand beside him.

"You're a horse whisperer?" he asked as they walked back to the house.

"A witch." She grinned.

They dined that evening on the terrace. Sofia had fixed a feast of lamb, boiled potatoes from the garden, fresh lettuce for the salad, and Vislogus wine from Syrah grapes. She understood now Torre's excitement at the winery as it was mellow and perfectly enhanced the meal.

She had changed into a sundress, gold with Southwestern patterns. She knew it was flattering, especially as the sun began to set and throw a red glow over the land. Mitch had changed into shorts and a tank top. The feelings she had, how she admired his virile body, her own body's reaction to his faintest touch, all of it was new to her. His voice was deep and when he laughed, it was as though he was touching her, even more when his gaze moved down her body, and his eyes showed he liked what he saw.

After they'd eaten, he pulled out her chair and took her arm to help her rise. She didn't need the help, but there was an old world courtliness about it that had her breathing a little faster. She followed him to a lower patio where they sat on lawn chairs, watching the sky do its thing.

Theirs was a companionable silence, as their energies merged and moved apart, all while not physically touched. She'd never been with a man who had equal spiritual power to hers, maybe even more. It seduced her as much as did his physical body—and that was saying a lot.

"They say we could get a storm tomorrow," he said sipping his wine and watching her over the rim of his glass.

"The land seems dry, so that is probably a good thing." She was trying to keep her thoughts on the mundane, like the weather. Instead, they were on the man across from her who sprawled in his chair with ease and yet there was leashed power. She could see him as a movie star or an Apache riding across this land. He showed his dual heritages in every move he made.

"I want to make love to you," he said. "I suppose that's not a good way to approach a seduction."

She smiled. "It's direct."

"You're not ready for that yet though, are you?"

"Are you?"

He laughed at that, rose, and refilled their glasses. "Maybe not the ramifications."

"Let's talk about who we are. You had an education. I should have known that from your book. Where was it?"

"Stanford. Other than my spirit guide, I had mostly been home educated, with a hunger to learn, by my grandfather and a trader, Josiah Taggert, who lived in Cibecue part of the year. That would have been the end of it, if at eighteen, my life hadn't been upturned, when my dying grandfather told me my father's name.

"I buried Grandpa, took the few dollars he had left me, and hitched my way to L.A. I didn't know if my father would care or believe me. I found he had an office in town where I left a message with someone who looked at me strangely. The call came that night. He sent a car to the cheap motel where I had just enough money to stay two nights. When I met him, it was obvious he was my sire." He gave a little laugh.

"I wasn't sure what that would mean to him, but it turned out, he'd not known about me or had any other children. He wanted to make up for what he'd lost. He flew me here the next day. We talked, much as you and I are. I didn't tell him then about my spirit guide, but maybe he knew. Anyway, he wanted to contribute to the man I would be. I took tests and got surprisingly high marks. With my father being who he was, Stanford let me in, and I did well there."

"What did you major in?"

"English, of course." He smiled.

"You got a degree."

"Master's."

"I started but quit at the end of my sophomore year. With no interest I wanted to pursue, it seemed a waste of time and money."

"Do you have such an interest now?"

She had to think about that. "I guess marketing, finding what others want to buy, and then solving mysteries. It doesn't take a college degree for that, just studying people and trends."

"And a natural talent."

She smiled. "Maybe some. Back to you. Did you write the book right after graduating?" She knew it hadn't come out then.

He shook his head. "Never gave it a thought back then. That came later."

"It's been a huge success."

"Depends on how you define success. The book cost me."

"By making you a target?"

He studied her before he answered. "It was more than that. My ancestor, Nantan Lupan, had been my spirit guide. He taught me a lot of what I know about the other side, about power, about how to use it." When he stopped, took a deep breath, she wondered if he'd go on. "He came to me after the book had come out and said I had done wrong by revealing the secrets of the unseen world. He said it will make things worse and for more than me. For the world. He's not come to me since."

"That's a terrible loss."

"It was. Maybe you understand then why I don't want to make it worse."

"And a play might do that?"

"It would add a dimension of reality. To speak of things unseen is asking for loss and attack. I've had both since I wrote the damned book."

"I guess I understand, but you don't hide what is out there by not writing about it. It's there. And some use it for their own gain, while others remain sheep and ignorant of how to protect themselves or how to fight it."

He let out a breath. "I see your point on that, but most won't believe it anyway. They saw *Vislogus* as entertainment and not real."

"You know better than that, as do I."

"Speaking of I... tell me more about you, about your family."

"We are natural born witches and shamans. My sisters and I have been trained not only in using what we have for gifts but also in martial arts. Even my grandmothers are still actively working magick, connecting to the other side, doing what they can to make the world better."

"How about beyond magick."

"You mean beyond spells and potions," she said with a laugh. "There is the boutique, of course. We help with Hemstreet Detective Agency when needed. You know I live in Barrio Viejo. I have been involved in protecting it from losing its character and being bulldozed by developers."

"And romantic interests?"

"You didn't tell me about yours." The night was darkening around them, and the sounds shifted to crickets, night birds, and frogs. An owl called from a distant cottonwood tree. She could hear the sound of the river even though it was far below the house. The fragrance of sage and juniper lingered on the night air, maybe even the grapes although she knew she had an enhanced sense of smell due to her training, her own wolf shifting, and her desire to feel all of what was around her. In the city, she lost some of that. She liked it here.

"I haven't been with a woman in over a year, and even then it was more her using me than me using her. Some think the book or my money is more important than who I am."

She considered that. "You are a very handsome man. That might've been more a factor."

He smiled. "You think so? I don't see myself that way."

"Women do, I would bet."

"You do?"

It was her turn to smile. "You are looking for compliments."

He smiled. "Of course."

"Well, then I find you handsome, but looks aren't everything, and for me I'd want something more before I became involved with a man on a physical level."

"Marriage?"

"Not necessarily but certainly commitment."

"I suppose you could cast a spell on anyone you wanted." He chuckled.

"There are those who believe that would work."

"Love potions." He smiled.

"Recently, when a young woman came asking for that, I tried to explain to her it doesn't work that way, but she wasn't able to comprehend—or didn't want to. It got me to thinking the world would be a better place if more understood magick."

"I doubt it."

"So you told me."

"I think it just brings the dark side to attack. It gives them a target."

"I guess that's possible."

"So, back to what's important..."

"And that is?" She knew that she was weakening. Maybe commitment wasn't so important as she had thought, at least in some situations. It was then that she felt the wind coming up. It didn't feel like a natural wind. "Do you feel that?" she asked.

He turned and looked toward from where it was coming. "This place has always been safe," he said as the gusts picked up.

"You did say a storm was coming."

"But this isn't it, is it?"

"Do you protect this place with wards?"

"I hadn't. I am not high on witchcraft even though..." He strode into the house and returned with a sword. She saw it glisten in the lawn lights.

"A sword?" she questioned as she rose and faced toward the source of the now gale.

"The metal is effective against demons." He looked at her then. "I might as well tell you. Your father made me this sword." He crouched down as something, no, it was someone came out of the darkness and pushed at him, backing off when it saw the sword.

"Not very friendly," a voice said. She recognized Ornis.

"Nor is raising up a tornado," Mitch said. "Are you out of your territory?"

"You thought I had limits. Uh, what's she doing here?" Ornis asked taking on more form and looking toward Elke.

"My guest."

Ornis laughed. "Is she encouraging you to take up arms against us?" He pointed toward the sword.

"Stop the wind, and we can talk friendly-like. Otherwise..." When Adolph growled, Mitch told the wolf to settle back and not get involved.

"Wise choice. I wouldn't want him hurt," Ornis said with a smirk.

"It might not end that way but leave him alone. He's not in this."

"By yourself, you want to take on the whole dark side?" Ornis asked with what sounded more like a cackle than a sincere laugh.

"Not particularly, but if required, you would be first."

"I haven't hurt you."

"You have encouraged others to hurt me and mine."

"Mine?" Again, Ornis looked toward Elke. "Is she now one of yours like your wolf?"

"While she's my guest."

It was then that Elke became aware of things falling around them. The table overturned. The glasses they'd been using fell and shattered. Flowers were torn from their stems.

Poltergeist.

She raised her arms and thrust energy toward where she knew the lower level demon was stirring up havoc. She heard it heading into the house and followed hoping that Ornis and Mitch would not fall to battle. That wasn't usually Ornis' style, but things were changing.

The lower level of the house had a family room and it was there that the poltergeist was breaking things and throwing them around. "Be gone," she commanded, putting out her hands and using energy to encircle the spirit, who fought back. Because it was a lower level spirit, it didn't have the power to stand against her for more than a few moments. Laughter was followed by its disappearance. She looked around the room. Using more of her energy, she restored what had been damaged. Although she'd dealt with poltergeists before, it was unusual for them to attack a witch. Ornis had to be reassuring them of his support.

She hurried back outside to see that Ornis had conjured a sword of his own and taken on more of a human shape, a warrior in chain metal as he clashed with Mitch in shorts and a tank top. The sounds of the swords meeting clanged again and again, before Ornis laughed and vanished into the ether, taking the wind with him.

CHAPTER 9

"What was that about?" she asked as she righted the overturned table.

"Showing me this place is not safe, I guess, but then why play games?"

"Was it just a game? Did you see the poltergeist?"

"I saw what it did, not it."

She considered that. What was Ornis up to? She'd thought of him mostly a nuisance, a demon who worked to use humans but had little real interest in direct battles. Now, she wasn't so sure. They needed to understand the plan. Had she been shepherded to meet Mitch, and it was all part of some larger design? The question of Ornis could not be instantly resolved. She had another one that maybe could. "Only my father could have given you that sword. Tell me about it."

"My father told me he was thinking of investing in a Tucson development plan. He met with yours about it and took me. When it was over, your father, pulled me aside, said there were things I needed to know that he could teach me. Maybe it's why my father had brought me although he wasn't into the supernatural—other than making people want to see his films maybe." He laughed. "Want a whiskey?"

She shook her head. She needed a clear head. He poured himself a shot from an outdoor cupboard. Returning to her, he sat on the lawn chair again. She moved to sit across from him. "I saw you then," he said.

"How?"

"You and your sisters came in. You were still a girl from. You haven't changed a lot."

"I don't remember."

"I imagine your father had many such meetings."

She laughed. "Not with big movie stars. I remember your father. He was a little older than our main heartthrobs of the time, but we were impressed. Dad shoed us out though. How old were you? I can't believe we wouldn't have noticed you."

"I kept a low profile around my father. I was sitting in a chair listening to the two men talk when you girls burst in."

"My sisters and I didn't realize how much of a wizard our father had been until recently. He kept that from us. We saw it as a female business, magick." She smiled at the memory.

"Well, he was very powerful. That's why it was such a shock when I heard he had been killed."

"To us also, but we can be killed, and he was riding a motorcycle, which can be dangerous, except he was skilled and not a risk taker. That night he had chosen to not wear a helmet for whatever his reasons. However it happened, reality is what we have to accept."

"Sometimes it is hard to tell the difference—between reality and what isn't."

She drew in a breath. "Maybe I do need that whiskey."

He smiled and went over to pour her a shot and refresh his. "So we have two problems," he said when he returned. "Finding out what Ornis really wants, who he is using, and then there is us."

"You mean-- whether there should be an us?"

"It's on my mind."

"You are plainspoken."

"Maybe it's why there've been so few women in my life." He laughed. "Women like flowery words, and I'm no good at them."

"I'm plainspoken too, so it's not a bad thing for me. I won't though get involved with you, beyond friends, until I know it is more than a one-night stand."

"Agreed." He smiled then. "How about kissing? Is that off limits too?"

She knew it was a mistake, but she said, "No, we could kiss." Almost before she'd gotten out the words, he reached for her and pulled her onto his lap. With his right hand, he brought her head to where their lips were a breath apart.

"I want to kiss you," he said, "but we might not be able to stop with one."

"Trust me," she said with a smile as she brushed his lips with hers, "I can."

He opened his mouth and brought their lips together. She closed her eyes, aware of the powerful surge she felt as his touch. Then his tongue went into her mouth, and her body reacted as his arms tightened around her. She'd never felt this reaction from a kiss, wanted it to last forever, and then knew she better end it.

She pushed back, a little out of breath. "I know what they mean about can't eat just one," she said with a teasing smile but moved off his lap and back to her seat. "I also know my limits."

"All right... for now." He let out a breath. "I won't stop trying to change your mind."

"I know. So let's talk about what will cool this off."

"You mean us or them?" He smiled.

"You know what I mean. Ornis and whoever else is involved in what was happening in Tucson and now here. You lied to me the first time I asked you if you knew him. What do you know about him?"

"I had run into him, yes, and when you asked, I didn't know much about you other than your father and desire to use my book." He sipped his whiskey. "He's a demon, of course. Not the highest level, but he influences those below him. Mostly he causes damage by the humans he can use, those who want power, and don't care from where it comes. All demons are malicious but..."

"You hadn't seen him as a serious risk."

"Not particularly, but I hadn't expected him to leave his normal territory and am not sure what this was about."

"Me either. I should call my mother tomorrow."

"To see what happened after you left?"

"Maybe more murders. I hope not, but whoever did that is trying to make it look like the earlier ones. Why would someone do that?"

"Maybe to distract from their own motive."

If that was the case, the logical one behind it would be Martin Jefferies. She saw by Mitch's expression that he recognized the possibilities. She worried then that her sisters were going to visit the church, disguised but still, was that safe. If, ironic as it would seem,

Ornis was behind the pastor there, then he would see through them. "I need to talk to my family."

"Phones or psychic connections?"

"There is less chance of misunderstandings if I call tomorrow."

"Your phone can be traced."

"So could my psychic vibes. And Ornis knows I'm here anyway."

"So call and see what they know. I bet it won't be good news."

She laughed. "They will wonder why I'm here."

"Tell them you got kidnapped by a madman. That'd be close anyway."

><><><

Mitch spent a restless night, sleeping but not well. In the morning, he fed Adolph and was drinking coffee, when Elke entered. "I should call," she said, "and see what has gone on there."

He nodded. "Eat first and then for privacy, at least from humans, you can call from outside if you wish."

Sofia handed over a platter of French toast. Elke ate hers with just butter, but Mitch added syrup. "Did you bring a swimsuit?" he asked as he drank a third cup of coffee.

"No, do I need one?"

He smiled. "Well not that I'd mind but you might—that is unless you've changed your mind on our discussion last night."

He saw her blush. He liked that. "Uh, there is a spot on the river wide enough for swimming?" she asked avoiding his comment.

"I had another place in mind. Call and I'll tell you more."

She smiled and went outside with her cell.

Adolph settled at his feet. 'Am I going with you?' he asked with thought patterns while Sofia was in the room.

"Not to Jerome," Mitch answered. He looked up to see the questioning expression on Sofia's face. "Just letting him know he's not coming with me today." He smiled. People talk to their pets-- that's the usual. It is pets talking back that was not. Although she knew the home wasn't exactly normal, she had never experienced how very irregular it was. She'd probably quit if she did, and he had valued her

98

service for too many years to take the risk. He would do what he could to keep her from seeing the worst of it. For that, he was grateful Elke had used her magick to clean up the prior night's happenings.

When Elke returned, she poured herself another cup of coffee.

"How is your family?" he asked gesturing with his eyes toward Sofia, hopefully to warn her not to get into the witchcraft side of it.

"I talked to Mom, and they are fine. They got the note I left with Luke." Her gaze met his levelly. "It's a lovely morning. Shall we take our coffee to the patio?"

He refilled his cup though he'd already drunk more than his usual. Outside, the morning air was warm, had enough breeze to cool it to the feeling of balmy tropics.

"No more murders," she said. "The demonstrators though have grown in number and are centering all their attention on the bookstore. They have even gotten a story in the newspaper with interviews as to their purpose. They are talking to customers to warn them the place is evil. Naturally, it has impacted sales."

"No violence though."

"Not yet, but Mom thinks that will come with this kind of fervor. She put up more wards, but they are intended for demons, not humans, who have lost touch with their spiritual side."

"Ironic. People believe what they are preconditioned to. Some supernatural abilities are fine. Others are not. My book or your play will change nothing."

"Not at this point with those people, but at an earlier point, it might. That has been my hope."

"You are a hopeless dreamer." He smiled to take the sting from his words.

"It's the dreamers who have hope."

"An unrealistic hope."

"You are a cynic."

"Only one of my many virtues."

She laughed. "Don't you mean flaws?"

"Would I admit that?"

"You might if you wanted to drive me off."

"Being a cynic would do that?"

"Oh no, that would attract me. Watch out."

"Let's go get you a swim suit. I have a plot, er make that plan."

"Maybe I have one of my own."

He grinned. "I can handle that... I hope." He didn't want to smile but couldn't hold it back.

><><><

An hour later, he had driven her up to Jerome. "Ever been here before?" he asked as he found a place to park the truck—not easy given there were already a lot of visitors and limited parking. She felt the energies and realized this town was full of ghosts. She wondered if Mitch knew that. While she knew he had powers, she wasn't sure which ones.

"No, this would be a first time, but I've heard of it."

"It's had a long history of mining. This is Cleopatra Hill, and are you interested in any of this?" He laughed when he saw she'd been distracted—what he couldn't know was why.

She saw a woman walk past wearing a long dress, with dark hair mostly hidden under a bonnet. Was she part of an historic reenactment? Then she vanished. She had seemed oblivious to Mitch and her —even though Elke was relatively certain the ghost knew they were there. Some ghosts had a hard time adjusting to not being human. If this woman had died in the period where her clothing fit, she'd had a very hard time. Being in places they had been when alive provided comfort until they could finally let go of one life—one probably unhappily lived or ended. Looking around, she saw more. She wasn't sure how aware the ghosts even were of one another. She saw some wearing rough clothing, maybe one-time miners.

"Do you see ghosts?" she asked when she looked back at him.

"*Chĭdn?*"

"Navajo call them *chindi*-- the bad ones anyway. Is *chĭdin* what Apaches call them?"

He nodded. "You wouldn't have asked if you didn't see some today."

"When I want to and especially places like this, where there are a lot. Maybe the tourists draw them or where so many may have died."

"They don't stick to cemeteries, huh?" he teased.

She ignored his attempt at humor. "They don't have rules for where they will be, but some places attract them more than others."

"Any Apaches among the ones you see?"

"Should there be?"

He shrugged. "The Yavapai mined here, then the Spanish for copper. Long before the first claim was filed in 1876, it had been used. Al Sieber, a retired cavalry scout for General Crook, filed the first American claim after seeing the existing mines. After that came more, including the first bordello, and the big mines. It's also had a history of union problems of the violent sort. Lots of violent or sudden deaths. There have been stories about ghosts here."

Her experiences with ghosts hadn't been scary, nothing like with demons. She didn't want to think about any of it on a sunny day in this interesting old town. "You really think I can find a swimsuit here?"

"At this boutique." He pointed to one storefront. "And if it doesn't work for you, I'll take you down to Cottonwood to the Walmart." He grinned. "Somehow I doubt there'd be ghosts there."

Half an hour later, they emerged. She had an animal print bikini she might never have bought, but Mitch's eyes let her know he approved. She also bought a flowing skirt to wear over it with a plain white gauzy top. "So what's next?" she asked.

"How about lunch?" When she nodded, he put his arm around her waist. "In honor of your tastes, I suggest the Haunted Hamburger."

She laughed. "I love hamburgers." Soon they were seated on a patio with a glass of draft beer. The valley spread out below, with buildings as well as the old mines to see. Beyond lay the Verde Valley and in the hazy distance the Mogollon Ridge. History mingled with nature and spiritual mysteries. What made someone decide to remain when their human form no longer sufficed for them? Mystery.

He pointed to the menu and the Haunted Burger. "This is good."

"My gosh. It is loaded. I don't eat this much in two days." She wondered how anyone go their mouth around layers of bacon, cheddar, Swiss, mushrooms, green chilies, grilled onions, guacamole and of course the burger. Making it a double added twice the meat, cheese, and bacon. Who could eat that much food? Apparently, Mitch as he ordered it along with a side of fries. She asked for a ghostly burger, asking to not add the cheese and bacon.

Sipping his beer, Mitch said when the waiter had gone with their order, "So tell me, is this building haunted?"

She smiled. "Is it supposed to be?"

"There are those stories."

"For instance?"

"When they began trying to turn this into a restaurant, it was claimed that the spirits caused workers problems, like taking hammers and hiding them. Doors slammed into faces. Some say they are still seen like a woman in a flowing dress and bonnet. You see any?"

"I did on the street but not inside or on the patio." She looked around to be sure. "Maybe they are out for a walk."

"I haven't wanted to see them. What good does it do? Can you help them go on?"

She considered that. "Besides a cynic, you are very practical minded."

"They probably go together."

"Along with being a recluse."

"Maybe.

"You're also an introvert, aren't you?"

He let out a snort. "Geesus, you weren't a psychology major, were you?"

She shook her head. "Mostly reading since. Detectives use a lot of psychology, when trying to determine motives. And I'm an extrovert."

"I would have never guessed." This time his smile was even more cynical. Their hamburgers came, and he ordered them each another beer although she'd barely finished hers. "Stop," she told the server. "Bring me water instead."

Mitch shook his head but nodded to the waiter and sent him off. "So, you like digging into people to figure out what makes them tick."

"You're the writer. I'd guess that also requires digging into people."

"In my case, not so much."

"You didn't write your book."

"Remember Hemingway?"

"Of course."

"He wrote what he had lived and knew. When he ran out of that, he was done."

"So you are Adolfo, but you didn't experience all he did."

"Didn't I?"

"Where? Not in Tucson."

"No, to avoid people searching out its actual location, I set it in an imaginary site."

"And where it happened is another secret."

"I could tell you sometime-- if you really cared."

It didn't actually matter to her. "So your skills are as a warrior." She already knew the answer to that also.

"With one focus. I don't want war and have done what I can to avoid that. It comes to me though—want it or not. Nantan was probably right."

"The..." She hadn't expected that. In the battle there were battles, almost supernatural appearing ones. The hero had supernatural skills such as she'd never imagined using. While she had seen the book as reality, where it came to the adventure part of it, she thought it had been enhanced to make it exciting. If he was telling the truth, she and her family had mostly dabbled into the supernatural. Their battles had been on a much lower level.

"You can't just stop and put an end to the attacks on you?"

"You don't retire," he said as the waiter arrived with his beer, and he took a healthy slug. "You get retired."

"That's fatalistic."

His smile was cold. "Goes with cynical, right?"

"What made you decide to write the book?"

"I don't honestly know. Call it an impulse. I wanted people to understand the reality out there. Except, of course, it became *Star Wars* or *Harry Potter* and readers and reviewers didn't understand. I don't think even you did. You went for the intellectual argument."

"Was there an Estella?"

"No, that was my one fictional device. It allowed bouncing the argument around, as to whether magical answers to conflicts were ever justified. My character could have had the argument all in his head, but it was more effective as a conversation."

"You are a writer than whether you admit it or not."

He shrugged.

"No woman then has ever known who you really are?"

"Do I?" He laughed, but it was without humor.

"Given what you've told me, how did you decide to write it all down?"

"Let's eat our burgers before they get cold. I have plenty of time to tell you the rest."

She was dying of curiosity, but he was right. She set to eating and consumed less than half before she felt stuffed. She did snitch one of his fries as she watched him finish his burger.

He paid, and they went out to walk down the sidewalk to the truck. "What I'd like to do," he said, "is take the horses up into the hills, then down along Sycamore Creek. There are some beautiful spots to camp, one in particular. It'd be a better place to get answers that we both want. There is a place where we can talk without being overheard by demons, or for that matter ghosts, who carry stories." He grinned.

"And that's where you'll tell me the rest of your story."

"If you are interested." His smiled turned crooked. "I warn you that I'll also try to seduce you."

It wouldn't take much. She was already half in love with him, maybe had been when she read his book. She needed though to understand who he was. Could he be a delusional schizophrenic? Then she remembered his brief fight with Ornis. No, whatever he was, if it was a delusion, she experienced the same one. The world, the so-called real world, wasn't at all what most humans thought. Why were some chosen to live with one foot in each world? She'd never had the answer to that question—nor to a purpose to her own life.

"When would we go?" she asked as she clicked her seatbelt.

"Early morning, right when the sun comes up to get the hottest part over first for the horses. When we drop down into the canyon, we'll have water, grass and shade for the rest of our ride."

"It sounds beautiful. I wish I'd brought my camera."

"I can loan you one."

"You don't want to take photographs?"

He smoothly took the curves going down off the mountain even when a motor coach was partly in his lane. "I don't do pictures," he said glancing over at her when they reached the main road where he turned left for his ranch.

"I did notice that. Is there a reason?"

"Of course," he said, with another of those enigmatic smiles. "Cameras steal your soul. Didn't you know?"

"Of course, I just forgot."

He chuckled. "So are you game for going?"

"I have a choice? You didn't give me one coming up here."

"Don't remind me of that." His smile was a little sheepish or maybe as close to that as his rugged face could manage. "I was overreacting. Sorry. Feel free to head back south. I'll even get you there."

It was her turn to smile. She could manage that for herself, as transporting herself was one of her developed skills—although this was farther than she'd tested it. The thing was-- she didn't want to go. "I'd like to see your special place. I find it hard to believe there is anywhere that safe though."

"This place at least *has* been. Here comes my cynicism. With our markings, the visits by holy men and women, its power has been enhanced. It's in a hidden slot canyon off Sycamore where most would not know of its existence."

"Did your father take you there?"

"My ancestor, Nantan. He was my guide, the one I told you about."

She heard the change in his voice. Pain was attached to what he'd told her. "Does this place have a name?"

He shook his head. "No. I suppose New Agers would call it a vortex."

"An energy place that enhances magick," We have visited those in Sedona."

"Yes, so you know they come in various energy patterns, some agree with us, some not so much. There are those that deflect demons. It isn't that the dark side doesn't know it's there. It's that they cannot enter. It was found by my people and then enhanced by the holy ones."

"We hiked into Boynton and went onto Bell Rock and Castle Rock but mostly just to see what we felt. The energy felt good but nothing that we can't find on our ranch in Tucson."

"You are right. Vortexes are many places. Some publicized." He turned onto the narrow drive that led to his ranch. "The ones that are protective are probably less known. Some don't believe in demons, of course."

She smiled at that. "Will we take Adolph?"

"Yes. Maybe not Ranger though. I'm considering that."

"I talked to him, and I think he understands now."

"How did you convince him?"

"My secret." She grinned, as he stopped in front of his home.

"I like his gait, and he's steady on steep places. I'd like to take him. Not to mention, other than Major, he's the one big enough to carry me. The stallion is a good mount, but can be dicey when the mares get in heat."

"Will I ride Pepper again?" she asked as they walked into the house.

"If you like."

"I do."

Sofia came out from the kitchen. "Will you be wanting lunch?"

"We had it in Jerome," Mitch said.

"Dinner then at seven?" she asked.

He nodded. He went to the sideboard and held up a bottle of wine. "Grenache okay with you?"

She hated to admit she knew little about wines and nodded. "Wonderful."

A few minutes later, she sniffed and then tasted the fruity wine. "I like this."

"It is mixed with Syrah. As I told you, I also don't know a lot about wine, which is why my vintner has to."

"Jacques Durand."

"Yep. I have had more interest in growing the grapes, finding the right places for them to flourish. The advantage of the Verde Valley is its diversity."

"You are a farmer then?"

"Looks like it." He sipped the wine. "I used to smoke. Still do sometimes, when the pressure builds, but it damages taste. Taste mattered to me. Something I wanted to develop." He watched her over the rim of his glass.

"And a witch suits your taste?" she asked with a little laugh.

"When she's beautiful and talks like you do."

"How do I talk?"

"A little throaty, warm, and then as though all the words matter."

"That is true on the last. It's what drew me to your book. It was the discussions, the arguments, the debate over whether someone had a right to use powers that others didn't have. And then, the question of why some? Why be born with these gifts? It wasn't as though my family asked for them."

"Someone in your family did."

"I suppose that is so. I hadn't thought of it that way. What about you? Were you born with them?"

"Can we save that answer for when we get to the safe place? You know as well as I that there is no privacy here."

"Wards help with that."

"I haven't used them."

"I know. I put one around the house when I arrived."

"Didn't keep Ornis away."

She laughed as she took another sip of the wine. "He was outside." The poltergeist, however, had come in, and although she'd forced it away, her ward hadn't blocked its entry. That worried her. Maybe Mitch's safe spot would be more powerful at repelling demons. She hoped so.

CHAPTER 10

At first light, Elke pulled on jeans, boots, a tank top, and a cotton shirt. She stuffed extra underwear, her new purchases, and a pair of sandals into a bag. She had no idea what to expect but added a pair of shorts. She'd sleep in her underwear, she guessed. Would he take a tent or was this to be really roughing it?

In the kitchen, Sofia turned to look at her with a smile. "He's already outside," she said. "I am fixing a stack of hotcakes. What would you like for breakfast?"

"Hotcakes are fine." She poured her coffee.

Sofia smiled. "He said you'll be gone a couple of days. I packed food for three with dry for Adolph. Hope that's enough." Elke had no idea. Camping is something she'd never done.

When Mitch came through the door, Adolph at his heels, he was wearing a plaid shirt that he'd ripped the sleeves from, Wranglers, boots, with a holster and gun belted to his hip. He threw his Stetson on the rack. "You need a gun?" she asked. She'd never owned one. Never fired one.

"Not usually but sometimes. There are rattlers up there, cougar, sometimes a bear. For the last two, it'd be making noise more than killing it—at least for the first shot."

He washed up at the sink, then with coffee, sat across from her. "I saddled the horses. I hope it's not a mistake taking Ranger."

"You can still change your mind." Sofia set a plate in front of each of them. Mitch put butter and syrup on his. She settled for a little butter. Mostly she avoided carbs, but the hamburger the day before had tasted good. Maybe there'd be a place to go for a run in the canyon—that is if it wasn't already too hot when they got there.

"We sleep up there, wherever up there is, for two nights?" she asked and shook her head at another hotcake when Mitch took more.

"More likely three, but we'll see. It'll take us half a day to get there. You won't get cellphone coverage in there. No point in taking it."

She didn't need the phone to contact her family, but she nodded and smiled. "What about the camera?" she asked.

He got up and retrieved it from a shelf. "Just no pictures of me."

She smiled innocently. "Of course not, I wouldn't want to steal your soul." She nodded when Sofia poured another cup of coffee.

"Is there a point at which we should send someone for you?" Sofia asked.

"If we're not back by the 29th, call Joe, and tell him to come up. He'll know where. We will be back though." He looked back at her. "Where's your bag?" She pointed to the chair beside the door. "I'll stow it. He also picked up the bag Sofia had packed with food. He pointed to hats on the rack. "If you don't have one, pick out one from there. Come out when you're ready," he said before he shoved his Stetson back on his head and left.

"Is he always like this?" Elke asked after a quick stop in the bathroom.

"Energetic, you mean?"

She laughed. "I guess that's what it is." She studied the hats to which he'd pointed. Trying on a soft cotton one with a sizeable brim, it would protect her from the sun and not be too heavy. Stetsons weren't really her thing—except on him.

"I worked for his papa. They are two peas in a pod." She gave an affectionate laugh. "Mr. Robert was so happy when Mitch came to him. They only had… I guess five years together, but they were good ones for Mitch's father. He'd gone through much hell before that."

"How long were you with him?"

She considered. "Twenty five years. I saw him through three wives. Two he lost due to his own recklessness. He was trying to build a career, which meant he was gone a lot. The last one, she was beautiful, like a siren, and like a siren, she was hell itself."

"She was already out of the home when Mitch came, I think he said."

"Regina and yes. She cheated on Mr. Robert, treated him bad, then got a big settlement because it was worth it to him to see her gone."

"And she had a son." She didn't want to pry, but she was interested in stories. This was a powerful one.

"Roger. Weak. Sad. Never enough for his mama or Mr. Robert. Then along came Mitch, who was all any man could want in a son. That woman hated him from the moment she saw him. He was all her son never could be."

"Do you still see them?" Had that segment of his father's life continued into Mitch's.

"Not up here, not sure how much in Tucson for Roger. Never her." Elke could see Sofia had become uneasy at discussing her employer.

"Do you have family around here?" she asked.

"A sister in Tucson. She's older, not in good health. Mitch has been good to her, as he is with many he helps."

"Well, have a nice vacation while we are gone." She stopped at the door. "You are a great cook by the way."

Sofia smiled broadly. "Thank you. It's a pleasure to cook for those who appreciate food.

Outside, Elke saw Mitch down by the barn. She was surprised to see he had tied most of the supplies on a third horse, a buckskin gelding. He looked up as she came to him. "I decided to take Traveler. It'll make this easier on the other two and just in case Ranger ends up not working out. I will say he seems calmer than he ever had around Adolph and me."

She walked to Ranger and rubbed his nose, then mounted Pepper. "How many hours to where we are going?" she asked as he swung into his saddle and took the lead rope in hand.

"Five or six. Not so far in one sense, but it's like another world."

They took a trail that led north from the ranch through dry grass, rabbit bush, cacti and mesquite. As the trail climbed, the vegetation added prickly pear. In the distance, she saw rock cliffs and far away were dark, pine covered mountains. Ahead of them loped Adolph, only looking back now and then to be sure they were still with him.

When the trail was broader, Mitch slowed Ranger, so he could ride beside Elke. "He's like a different horse," he said. "I'd like to know what you told him." He laughed.

"Our secret... for now."

"Do you have a lot of those?"

"I think not as many as you. You have had me wondering ever since you said that about the book."

"And I told you when it's where it's safe, where we can put together all the pieces of the puzzle, I'll tell you."

"I can wait." She was curious though, and her mind went in circles trying to reason it all out.

"I have a question for you."

"Okay."

"You see ghosts. Is my father hanging around the ranch?"

"I haven't seen him or any ghosts at the ranch. You know are eager to reincarnate. They can still be called, but they are forming new lives."

"Do you have the ability to see where or what that might be for him?"

"Maybe. I think I told you that my powers can't be for idle curiosity."

"I suppose it would be that. He came into my life late and yet was important to me. He got me what I needed and without my ever asking."

"Then he had his own powers."

"I guess that's what it was. I'd like to think he's happy wherever he is."

"I wish I could tell you." She could probably if she put energy into it, but would that be a misuse. She was very cautious in how she used power. Maybe she'd been too cautious considering the world in which they lived.

"The air smells good up here," she said.

"You can begin to smell the mountain and the canyon."

"You said wild animals."

"We might see ring-tailed cats, black bears, mountain lions, peccary, and of course, watch out for rattlesnakes, scorpions. Sometimes deer and seasonally elk. Lots of birds, canyon wrens and hermit thrushes. The biggest problem is mosquitos though." He grinned when she gave him a look of concern. "It's why I brought repellent." He patted his saddlebag.

"I'm glad to hear that."

"Wards don't work on them?"

She giggled. "Maybe I should try, but not sure they're the type of demon it's designed to block."

"Just in case they aren't, I also brought a tent with mosquito netting."

"For both of us?" She debated the meaning of that. How easy would it be to resist him if he was determined? He appeared to be the sort of man used to getting what he wanted.

"I am used to sleeping out. It's for you... Unless..." His smile turned soft and tempting. "You invite me in."

She ignored that because she was unsure what to say. "I can see the canyon in the distance, but how do we get into it? You don't take the usual route, do you?"

"No, we go in farther up on an old Yavapai trail. Not that steep, but we'll take it slow."

"You are White Mountain, aren't you?"

"You know the tribes?"

"A little. I know the area around Cibecue is White Mountain." She laughed. "Okay, given I've lived in Arizona all my life, I know little about the Apaches beyond Geronimo and Cochise."

"And with them most likely the stereotypes." He edged Ranger back to paying attention. She hoped the gelding would stick to what he'd said. So far, he seemed calm, even when Adolph loped near.

"Probably," she admitted.

"Mountains are important to my people. Did you know that?"

Thinking of her name and the mountain names of her sisters and mother, she should have known it, but she hadn't about the Apache. She shook her head.

"We have many that are sacred, with the different tribes having different ones based on where they were based. In Arizona, Mount Baldy is probably most significant. For the White Mountain tribe, the White Mountains, of course, Pinaleno up near Safford, then the four peaks in Phoenix in the Superstitions, and the San Francisco Peaks. The belief is the higher you go on a mountain, the better your medicine will be. Mountains are places for healing."

"And this canyon, what is it about it?"

"It's one that is not only sacred to me, but some consider it to have been a place of aliens."

"Seriously? Aliens?" She laughed.

"It's no joke to those who claim they were kidnapped by them."

"Do you believe in that?"

"Apaches base their religion on two things—the supernatural and the power of nature. I believe Sycamore Canyon provides both of those."

"You didn't answer me."

"I know." Conveniently, for him to avoid answering, the trail narrowed, and he went ahead. "Don't forget to drink water," he said turning in the saddle. "Dehydration can catch you off guard when it's as hot as this."

She glanced to the south. "I worry more about storms. Not good up here if we are caught in one."

"We'll be in the canyon by then."

"Uh what about flash floods?" she asked, looking over her shoulder. It would have been good if her psychic abilities included reading the weather.

"We'll be in a side canyon and above any risk. Hey, quit worrying. I've got this." He gave her an encouraging smile, but she was relieved he picked up their pace a little. The trail wound over hills and into shallow draws. Finally she saw what she guessed was the trail down. From what she could see, it sounded as if he had accurately described it, and they started down.

Half an hour later, they were riding along the creek. The storm clouds continued building overhead, but she saw no lightning-- yet. At this time of year, it was inevitable. She felt relieved when he took the horses across the creek at a shallow crossing and headed into a canyon that had been almost invisible until they were riding into its narrow cut. A small creek was alongside the less developed trail, but the horses handled it with no stumbling. When the canyon opened, she saw beautiful red walls, a small waterfall, and a pool. Better yet, there was tall grass for the horses.

She unsaddled Pepper as he took care of Ranger and removed the packs from Traveler. "It's your job," he told Adolph, "to keep them from heading down canyon. There is plenty of food here." He looked at Ranger especially. "And oats for the well-behaved." The mare and geldings looked at the wolf with interest but did not appear threatened. After getting a drink from the stream, they started eating the grass.

"What can I do to help?" Elke said joining Mitch where he was unpacking their supplies.

He handed her a wine bottle and opener. "Can you handle this?"

Smiling, she took it and got the bottle open by the time he handed her two plastic cups. She saw he had packed a small table, which he unfolded along with two chairs. "This is fancy camping," she said as she set his wine and the bottle on the table.

She looked around as she sipped the wine. The walls were reddish orange with interesting shapes. "Over there," he told her, "are petroglyphs. Ever seen them?"

"In Tucson." She walked to the smooth cliff face to study etched and painted symbols. A few looked fresher than she'd have expected.

"The pictographs are Apache. The petroglyphs are the Sinagua who came first... so far as it is known."

She recognized a Kokopelli image, some snakes, a man on horseback and then mountain goats. The painted ones were shields with zigzag patterns. The latter reminded her the sky had turned very dark and looked like rain was on its way if not lightning with it. She looked back to the campsite to see Mitch attaching a tarp to the nearest cottonwood. Soon he had it stretched to a willow and another tree she couldn't identify.

She put out her feelers to sense if there were any spirits in the canyon. As he had said, she felt nothing but a peaceful energy. Whether the spirits would show up, she didn't know, but she put out some of her own wards as an extra protection—hoping if lightning came, it would help with that too. She felt safe there, any lightning bolts likely to hit the rim. She swatted a mosquito that had landed on her arm.

"Use some repellant," Mitch said, taking a little bottle from his shirt pocket. "Dot it a few places and they'll leave you alone." She did that, not minding its musky odor as much as she'd expected, and the mosquitos moved back.

She watched as he opened up an orange tent. He had said she'd have it to herself. She wasn't sure she wanted that. She watched his muscles move as he pounded in pegs. Soon using the poles, he had it erected under the tarp. He threw in one sleeping bag with the other outside. With a small device, he inflated one air mattress.

She heard the rain hit the tarp and watched as it fell in the canyon. "That should send the mosquitos off for a while," he said as he stood and looked around their small camp. A two-burner propane stove was on the table. "Want some coffee or are you ready for supper?"

"What is supper going to be?" she asked as he took packets from a sack.

"Your choice. Chicken and dumplings, beef stroganoff, beef stew, chili, or spaghetti?"

"All that in those little packets?"

"Dehydrated and better tasting than you might imagine."

"Then I choose spaghetti."

He took out a black device with a handle and hose. "Ever seen one of these?"

"Nope."

"it's a Katadyn Vario and simple to use. This hose with a prefilter would take out any sediment, which there is not in this pool." Ignoring the rain, he took it, their now empty water bottles, and a pan to the pool. She watched from the shelter of the tarp.

"I put the hose into the pool, pump this handle and the water flow starts going through the filter. It can filter two quarts, safe to drink, in a minute." He refilled the water bottles and then the pan. "I could drink from the pool, have many times, but you haven't. Giardia would put a damper on our trip. So you stick to drinking the purified."

"You do this a lot I can tell," she said admiring the smooth way he took care of everything. With the gun on his hip, he looked as though he belonged in this canyon from centuries past. It was his element. As she considered that, she consulted the canyon's earth Elementals, felt their pleasure at his returning to their land. She was pleased at their welcoming of her. No wonder bad spirits stayed away. It was protected by many years of shamans making it so.

"When I come here, it's with one horse, a sleeping bag, jerky, biscuits, water bag, and a bottle of whiskey." He chuckled. "I thought you'd enjoy our time here more with a few refinements."

"You're right. I've never camped at all, but I knew some did it." She smiled.

"Seriously? Never? Hard to believe. Your father was an outdoorsman."

"But Mom was not. I guess he did his thing without his girls unless maybe he took Torre. She's the most outdoors oriented of us. I should ask her. Dad was good at helping us each do our thing."

"Well, I hope you enjoy being here. It's the one place I knew we could talk without being overheard, and now, the storm seems to be passing."

"Until the next one. I wondered... were you still in touch with him when he was killed?"

"No. Before my father died, Marcus told me he'd given me all he had, and it was up to me." He gave a little laugh as he poured himself another glass of wine. "I didn't understand what he meant then. I do now."

An hour later, they'd eaten the spaghetti, and it was better than she had expected. After checking on the horses, he opened another bottle of wine. "Time to talk," he said, surprising her. The storm clouds had passed, but the light was beginning to fade as the sun went behind the canyon walls.

"After your father died, is that when the events in *Vislogus* occurred?" she asked wondering if he had been teasing earlier when he'd said the book hadn't all been fiction.

He laughed. "Isn't it your turn first to reveal your secrets?"

"My life isn't nearly as interesting from the sounds of it. A normal childhood, until my father was killed anyway, normal as much as possible for a family of witches, college for two years, then working in my mother's detective agency until Torre and I opened Mellow Yellow."

"You were young when he was killed."

"Fifteen. I wish now I'd known him as you did. He left our spiritual training to our mother and grandmother's. He was busy with finance and development. It was only this year that my sisters and I realized he had been a wizard. I notice, by the way, that you did bring your sword up here."

"I trust-- but not completely." He smiled. "And yes, your father made it for me if I hadn't already told you that."

"When he was killed, Mom had to take over his businesses. That's when I became more involved in them. We have the boutique, but Torre and I also help Mom. Torre is gifted in computers. I help out with business decisions. We have several in Tucson where we're silent partners—luckily as things stand now. Mom has little interest in business details—especially the anal stuff. Denali had more interest in the arts. Devi... well, not sure what she likes. She just does what she must, I guess. She's shy and quiet."

"You are also into theater."

"As a backer. I wanted to use your book, well, not all of it. The action part would be impossible for a small theater. But the argument, which was made, with ironic humor I might add, that magick can be used for good or ill, that we all have some of it if we so choose, was something more need to hear."

He let out a breath. "That is really Apache philosophy. I was brought up with that engrained and especially by Nantan Lupan."

"You gave your hero his last name."

"It did not go over well with him, as I told you. He has yet to forgive me. He did not want our secrets revealed that way. He said I would make a target of myself. It turned out he was right, except, I'd already been a target."

"Because of what my father taught you?"

"Among other things probably. It was in Mexico that most of what I described in *Vislogus* happened. That conversation you want to use was not actual, but it was the argument I had with myself over it all. Being only half Apache, even knowing what I had experienced with the spirit world, I still questioned my sanity. It's one reason I chose to call it fiction, not memoir."

"Tell me about the Apache religion. I know so little."

"The tribes vary, but I was taught don't use peyote, as dreams are how we are reached by the *others*. Power is given through plants, animals or natural phenomena like say a whirlwind. Often one is chosen and accepts the power after a ritual that is an ordeal. That is how the sun dance came to be."

"Do you believe people are born to mysticism or acquire it?"

"Some maybe are more open to it based on their families. Apaches believe we have the potential to have many powers, as we need them. Powers must be used for the common good or that person is considered a witch." He gave her a crooked grin.

"We have a bad press," she agreed.

"I guess all spiritual power has that unless it is from the right god, and even then it has to be proven or death can be the result."

The sky had turned crimson as the sun finally turned it into one fantastic lightshow as it disappeared for another day. Overhead the first stars were beginning to show up. "How fantastic," she said staring at their emerging patterns. "I guess it's being higher, and no other lights to distract from them."

"And a new moon."

"That too." She thought then about him, about how he'd become the man he was. A woman would have to be strong to walk at his side. She smiled, as she knew the direction her thoughts were traveling. It was toward a more permanent relationship than she'd imagined wanting with any man—or than was probably on his mind.

"You are so beautiful tonight," he said brushing her cheek with his finger. "Want me to build a little fire. It's cooled off enough, I think."

"I'd love that if it's okay for this place."

"I've yet to receive a complaint." He gathered small branches. Using his own power, he lit the flame. "If it'd been anyone but you," he said, "I'd have used a match."

She laughed. "I am cautious also about my secrets."

"I wasn't when I wrote the book."

"Why did you?"

He shook his head. "I've asked myself that question many times. It poured out of me. The experience seemed it had to be shared and yet sharing made it all worse. I didn't expect it to cost me Nantan. I have continued to hope he would come back to me. He hasn't since."

"Maybe he has reincarnated."

"Maybe." She could see he doubted it.

She told him then about her family, the shamans, the witches, and their need to use what they could do for good. "In that we are like the Apache, I guess, but we claim the title witch proudly."

"I can't let you use the scenes."

"A little selfish, don't you think?" She smiled to soften her words.

"It might seem that way, but it's not because I want to keep it for myself. I can't undo what I've done, but I don't want others being made into targets."

"I understand that better now."

They sat in a companionable silence with the night closing around them and the small fire a glowing center of life and energy.

"I've asked myself what brought us together," he said finally.

"I suppose I was a little in love with Adolfo from the time I read the book. Maybe meeting him was more why I wanted to create the play."

"But back then he was fiction."

She laughed. "Was he?"

"So now what? Do you have a plan for what comes next? You

know what I want to come, but it won't happen unless you want it too."

"I don't do flings."

"Neither do I."

"Tell me about Estella."

He laughed. "I told you she was made up."

"Was she?"

"That's what I once thought." This time his smile set her body on fire.

CHAPTER 11

He wondered what she was thinking as she watched him. He felt as though she saw through his clothing, through his flesh, straight into his soul. It was frightening and exhilarating all at the same time.

"Estella seemed imaginary to me," he said finally, as he knelt in front of her chair and reached out to tangle his fingers in her hair. "Now I wonder."

"At what?" She stroked down his neck to his shoulder and then began unbuttoning his shirt.

"Maybe from the time I saw you as a girl, when you were much too young, and I wasn't ready. I knew from then-- somewhere you were out there."

"You didn't go looking for me." She opened his shirt and slid it off his shoulders. Running her fingers down his chest, his body felt electrified, as he grew hard.

"I didn't think it'd be fair." He rose then and lifted her into his arms, settling back down on the other chair with her cuddled in his lap. "To be honest, it made me angry when you showed up."

"I noticed."

"You didn't know the reason though." He bent forward and lightly brushed her lips with his.

She opened her mouth and deepened the kiss. "I don't read minds except when I must. I try not to be invasive."

"I'm in the mood to invade something."

"Are you prepared for that?"

He smiled. "Maybe not emotionally, but physically. I brought something for protect but wasn't going to pressure you."

"As you can see, you don't have to."

He kissed her again and felt her fingers against his skin. She touched him places he'd only dreamed of having a woman touch. It wasn't as though he'd never made love, but this went beyond anything he'd known. It was as though they were connected on levels beyond the flesh. He lowered her to his sleeping bag and stripped off her clothing as she took off his. "God, you are beautiful," he whispered against her breast.

She smiled and pulled him down for another kiss where her tongue danced with his. Within moments, he'd sheathed himself in the condom and felt her readiness for him. When he entered her, he stopped for a moment, trying to get control of himself. She was tightening around him, her legs had come up behind his buttocks, and he lost any chance of waiting, as she thrust up. The moments went beyond time, and he lost track of anything but her.

When she cried out, he felt his own climax and was with her. Afterward, he flopped back, feeling physically drained. He looked over to be sure this was still what she had wanted. She was smiling. In the faint light of the dying fire, he watched her walk to the pool to wash. He followed. It wasn't deep, only up to his thighs, but the water was cooling and felt good.

From the bank, Adolph was watching them. He wondered what his wolf thought.

"She will make a good mate for you," Adolph said in answer to that question.

"You will scare him off," Elke said coming out of the pool and letting her body dry in the warm night air.

"I don't scare easy," Mitch said as he stood beside her.

"We'll see. I can be pretty pushy if you hadn't noticed."

He laughed and walked up to their camp where he pulled on his shorts. He stuck a few branches onto the fire and built it up. Then he watched as she dressed. He noted Adolph doing the same thing. For the first time, he wondered if Adolph wanted a mate. He wasn't sure what that would involve, as he was a wolf, but something more than a wolf at the same time.

"Making love settled nothing," he said feeling a need to say something and knowing that sounded stupid—even to him.

"Was it supposed to?" She wrung out her wet hair before sitting back in her chair.

"I don't know. Was it?" He had zero experience in relationships with women. Did what they had done mean they were in a relationship?

"Look," she said, "don't worry about this. We had a momentary lapse, a weakness. I don't expect anything from you."

He pulled her out of the chair and into his arms. "Expect this. It won't be the only time it happens."

She laughed. "Well, we'll see about that."

"I don't think it's safe to be seen as my mate for now."

She shook her head. "For a writer, you don't exactly have a gift with words, do you know that?"

"I think I mentioned it a time or two."

"All right, so that's settled. Now, should we try to come up with a plan or go to sleep?"

"I wish I thought a plan was possible."

"First things first. I am tired. So let's talk in the morning." With that, she crawled into the tent and didn't invite him to follow.

"You handled that well," Adolph said with a wolfish smirk.

"I noticed."

When Elke woke in the morning, she felt more energized than she had in months or maybe years. She didn't know where it was going with Mitch, but she felt comfortable with where it was. She smelled coffee and dressed quickly in shorts and a tank top. After the night's rain, the air felt clean and fresh. She noticed for the first time that at the edge of the pool a few Indian paintbrush were blooming, a yellow flower she didn't recognize on the other side. The cliff edges were a beautiful red, washed by the rainfall and the pool a rich turquoise reflecting all the colors above it.

"I can understand why you love to come here," she said as handed her a cup of coffee.

"It has good memories." Squatting down, he put a pan filled with bacon over the flame. "Even more now." He smiled up at her. He was wearing shorts but no shirt. She had to look away to stop her traitorous body from reacting to all those muscles.

Adolph watched them. "I suppose you two go for a run when up here." She knew she could use one.

"I catch a rabbit when I can," Adolph said companionably. "Mitch doesn't care for them raw."

She laughed. "Me neither. Maybe though we could catch one and bring it back to cook." She realized then what she'd said and looked over to see Mitch watching her.

"You shift?" he asked his eyes darkening.

"When there is a need."

"To a wolf?"

"Of course. What else? It's what reassured Ranger when I told him."

Mitch snorted. "You could have told me."

"I was going to when needed. I actually thought about surprising you, but thought that might go badly." She laughed. "I am not as good at communicating as a wolf as Adolph is. You might've thought I was an enemy."

"I'd have gotten your scent. Now that I think about it… maybe I did." His smile had a wolfish look to it.

They ate, she took another cup of coffee, and then she said, "I guess it's time for us to discuss what we've been avoiding."

"Tucson." He sipped his coffee as he looked toward the pool. "I had hoped it would come to me up here—the answer."

"Who was it you fought when in Mexico? The ones in the book?"

"They were monsters brought there by Azaziel. I guess you know him."

"My family has had experience with him but lately it's all been Ornis."

"Sometimes I think Ornis is just a distraction. Then I wonder if I am underestimating him. I don't think he can control monsters. Azaziel either can, or he creates them. It was happening there in a mountain village, where the ones living there were at their mercy. Pretty much it was as I described in the book—a larger than life bear, what appeared to be a wolf—only bigger, and a huge woman, only she didn't look much like any woman I've seen."

She wondered why she hadn't recognized that the roughly described creatures had been the monsters of Native American mythology. She'd never seen them, but she'd read enough that she should have recognized them in his book. "You didn't have Adolph with you, did you, or did you just not put him into the story?"

"He left me behind," Adolph said with a displeased growl. "He should have taken me."

"I didn't know what I was going to find," Mitch reminded him. "I didn't want to take the chance of losing you."

"How did you get drawn in? Was it like the book?"

"More or less. A friend from university told me something was going on there, to the villagers, to his family, and it was getting worse. He asked my help because he knew I'd had some other encounters and had powers but not necessarily what kind. Before I got there, my friend had been killed. I had to find out what had happened, and from that point, there was no turning back."

"The sword, plasma bolts, and... what was the way you moved? Surely that can't be real?"

He smiled. "You'd be surprised when you face that kind of situation. The sword could kill demons, and it turned out monsters. I wasn't alone. Nantan was with me. I described him in the book as a spirit guide and didn't give out who he was to me-- or his name."

"What I hadn't experienced is how you could track them."

"I could and can." His smile was a little twisted.

"Humans don't walk on air," she observed still having a hard time with what didn't seem real in her own experience. She knew she could disappear and reappear but the gymnastics-- that she had never seen.

"Nor do humans throw energy bolts or use a sword forged by a wizard," he said. "Catapulting through the air is less interesting than it sounds. More like transporting, excepting of a real body. The monsters were confused. The ones I came across there weren't overly intelligent. The only one that got away was the big wolf. He vanished and so far as I know, hasn't been seen again."

"Rugaru."

"You know the monster stories?"

"Enough to know they aren't all myths. I know it from being told, not from seeing for myself. I know some of our horror movies come from them. Rugaru though is clever as the stories go. And there is not just one. And you took them all on by yourself."

"I had Nantan to guide me—so not totally alone. If I'd known before I went there, what I'd be facing, I might've stayed in Los Angeles." He smiled. She didn't believe him. He'd have still gone.

"It's not the first time I've heard of monsters reappearing... in reality, not fiction."

"I guess it is bound to happen now and again. When they think they can build up power. It can happen any place. In Mexico, they had been drawn by the demons. I guess I made it clear in the book that I didn't see a reason for it on their end. Anyway, I was some stove up afterward. Rugaru may be imaginary in books, but in reality, he can draw blood. When I was recuperating, the idea for writing about it came to me... as fiction, of course, but I wanted to warn people. Stupid idea, of course."

"I think it's noble."

He laughed at that. "You know I still don't like talking about it and regret I wrote the damned book. To be honest, the chills it sends down my spine is why I didn't want to talk about this in Tucson or at the ranch, but only where I believe there is some protection-- if there is such a place."

"So far as I know," she argued, "such monsters have long waited in wilderness areas. They have tried to build their power back by assorted methods, like energy vortexes, but someone has always come along-- like you. When they kill people, as with Wendigos, they suck their power. You stopped that."

"You know more about this than you have admitted."

"The stories are out there, and we work with a spirit guide who had some encounters in Montana."

"Then you understand why I've felt as I have."

She sighed and finished her coffee. "You feel they will come after you?"

"Or those close to me. That's what Nantan said. I had made myself a target."

"If more knew, you'd be less a target."

"Baby, people don't believe. They like fiction where it comes to monsters."

"All right. I understand more now."

"You witches have enough power to take on something like that?"

"We haven't had to… so far, but I hope we would."

"Hope is a pathetic word."

She smiled at that. "Sometimes it's the only word. Hey, want to go for that run? I need to work off the pancakes I ate the other day." She laughed and ruffled Adolph's coat.

He considered that. The horses would stay with the feed and water. It probably wouldn't hurt for them to take a run. He couldn't say he was coming up with any brilliant ideas sitting around the campfire.

She smiled as she began stripping. In moments, she had changed form into a wolf. Actually, a very beautiful female wolf. He could see Adolph showing interest. Quickly, he dropped his shorts and shifted himself. He hadn't thought of Adolph as competition. He had been his best friend and a pet—except, he was also very much a male. A male, now running in circles to show off for Elke, while she watched with a wolfish smile. Mitch felt annoyed at their silliness. Then he realized what he was feeling was jealousy.

'Remember,' he warned, 'stay away from humans. Some carry guns, and wolves are not considered their friend.'

She nodded and took off at a lope followed closely by Adolph. Mitch brought up the rear not liking it much. Hell, this had been a terrible idea—then he remembered it hadn't been his. For the first time, he considered getting a mate for Adolph. Or had his wolf found one?

When Elke got to the stream, she hesitated, and Mitch took over the lead. He scented what was around and appreciated how much more attuned he was when in wolf form. Humans had hiked this way only a few hours earlier, right after first light. They had been in a hurry with long strides. The way the tracks cut into the trail, they had the weight of men. They didn't hesitate at the cut, which means they weren't Apache. The fact that they were moving so fast made them seem unlikely to be the average hiker. What were they after? He glanced back at Adolph and Elke. They showed the same concern. Curiosity made him turn to the direction from which the men had come.

There was something strange in the air. He recognized it.

'Blood,' Elke sent. 'Something has been killed.'

They loped toward where the smell was growing stronger. The body was that of a woman, torn and ripped as though with teeth but larger teeth than theirs. He looked for footprints but saw nothing except now theirs. He'd have to eliminate those. 'You two go back to the canyon, while I take care of this,' he ordered. They both looked defiant, but when they saw his determined expression, they didn't argue and ran off.

Mitch morphed into a human form and spent time erasing all their tracks. He studied again the body. Had the men heading north done this? Had they come across it and run for their lives? He moved to the stream and washing off, he decided, naked or not, better he stay human as he headed toward their canyon. He felt uneasy as he loped from wading to the sandy beaches.

At the camp, Elke was back in her human form and dressed. Adolph was watching as he approached. "Why didn't you return to your wolf form?" he asked.

"I wanted to see what was happening from my own perspective." He pulled on his shorts.

"You know what it was," Elke said.

"Rugaru or something who wanted it to appear it was it."

"Should we report it?" she asked. He saw she was shaking. Maybe that was normal for her after shifting. It did take energy. He poured them each a shot of whiskey. When Adolph looked at him expectantly, he put food down for him, and the wolf eagerly gobbled it up.

"And what would we say? We saw this body while out as wolves? I erased our tracks but did you notice there were none ahead of us? Not even hers."

"Something dropped her there?"

"Or planted her." He didn't feel as secure in his canyon, as he had remembered, but then in the past, he'd had less enemies.

"Come here," he said as he sat on his chair. He didn't know if he expected her to obey, but she did and settled onto his lap.

"Rugaru could do it or something like him." She threaded her fingers through his hair, taking out the knots.

"Would he have followed me from Mexico, waiting here?"

"It seems unlikely." She took a sip of her whiskey. "You know it's just a name for them. Maybe one has always lived in these canyons."

"Always some have disappeared in this canyon, but then that happens in wilderness areas."

"It feels safe in here. The horses aren't acting nervous."

"The problem will come when we leave." He considered how they should go. At least he had his sword, which could kill the monster—if that's what it was. "And there were those men who were moving fast."

"I can shift into a raven," she offered, lightly kissing his temple, "if you want me to look for them."

"Are you joking? You think I'd take that risk with your life?"

"It'd be safe enough."

"If those men have guns, you are kidding yourself."

"All right, bad idea."

"My bad idea was bringing you to my ranch and then up here. I didn't think this would happen."

"Mitch, I wanted to come, wanted to be with you. We can beat whatever it is—together." She bent and claimed his lips with a kiss that reached into his soul. He didn't know if he believed she was right, but he wanted to.

Without discussing the body or figuring out what they should do, they spent a quiet afternoon. She put on the bikini she had bought and took a shower under the waterfall. The water felt delightful. Avoiding polluting the pristine pool, she used handfuls of sand to wash her body and hair. She wished Mitch would have joined her, but he was deep in thought.

She got the camera from her pack and took photos of the canyon, the waterfall, wildflowers, pool, Adolph, and the horses. She wished she could photograph Mitch as he sat on a large rock, oblivious to all around him. He was so beautiful, if that word worked for such a rugged looking man. Staying true to her promise, she resisted the temptation.

As the sun began to set, he fixed another of the dehydrated dinners and opened a new bottle of wine. "Tomorrow we should go back," he said. "I wish I had worked out something here but…"

"We can't leave that poor woman's body out there."

"I know. I am thinking."

"I can let my mother know, and she can notify the authorities," she said.

"There is no cell coverage in here."

She smiled. "It isn't needed either. Not for our communication."

"How would she tell the authorities without giving away our secret? It's not as though shifting into wolves is that believable."

"Or talking wolves," Adolph added with one of his smiles.

"What if the two of you start down the trail toward where we came in, and I will ride to the body with an excuse for finding it that I was out for a ride."

"Why don't I go with you?" she protested.

"Because I want Adolph long away from here with no possible accusations that it was him who killed the woman. I think you should also take Ranger. I don't have much confidence in how he'd react to the kill site. I'll ride Traveler."

"What if the killer is still there, watching, waiting?" She didn't like the idea of him going alone and yet she saw the logic to it. Adolph could not be seen anywhere near the body.

"I am giving you the gun," he said. "I hope you can shoot."

"Not a chance. I have my own weapon, remember." She managed a smile despite her uneasiness.

"I just wish I had someone to send with you."

"Perhaps me." The old voice came from the darkness. Although Elke had never heard it before, she knew who it had to be.

"Grandfather," Mitch said. She heard the relief in his voice.

The old man became clearer until he looked like a person of flesh and blood. His features were Native American, that of an old man—obviously his choice, as guides could look as they chose. He looked over at Elke and back to Mitch. "You hooked up with a witch?" he asked with a teasing smile.

"Her skills come in handy," Mitch said. "I have missed you."

"I know."

"Why did you stay away so long? Were you angry with me?"

The old man shook his head. "You didn't need me."

"I thought I did."

"No, you did fine."

"You aren't angry about the book?"

"No, but I worry about you. I don't want you to join me on the other side any sooner than is meant to be."

"Me either."

"So now, what do you want of me?"

"Go with her and Adolph, make sure they get safely back to the ranch and guard them, in case this turns worse."

"You know what this is?"

"I am guessing Rugaru followed me up from Mexico and wants revenge for his friends."

The old man walked into their camp and sat in one of the chairs. Though Elke knew he could have floated where he wanted, he had totally taken on a human form that looked very solid and surprisingly powerful. She was impressed, with hundreds of questions for him, but this was Mitch's guide, not hers.

Nantan looked back at her with another of those quixotic smiles. "And you, daughter of your mother and father, with the strength of them and your grandmothers—what do you want to know?"

"Is this the same Rugaru as Mitch confronted in Mexico or has this one lurked here outside the protected canyon and been here for centuries?"

Nantan chuckled and looked at Mitch. "Beautiful and smart. Adolph was right. She's a worthy mate for you, grandson. Don't let foolish doubts cause you to lose her." He then looked back at Elke. "It is not the same one. The one in Mexico went farther south to Central America to stir up what he can there. Someone wanted this one here."

"A demon?"

"Someone."

"Why did he kill the woman?" Mitch asked his expression dark.

"I don't waste time trying to sort out the logic of monsters—some of whom have none. I can guess though."

"And that would be?"

"She was with two men. They ran when they saw what attacked her. They will be afraid even to admit what they saw. Who would believe them? Perhaps they were cowards, but then they had no tools to take down one such as him." He looked back at Elke. "You do."

"You mean I should do it?" Elke asked, as Mitch simultaneously snapped, "Not a chance."

"He will run from you," Nantan said looking back at Mitch. "He's had instructions."

"And that is?"

Nantan shrugged and looked back at Elke. "Perhaps, she was to be drawn here and killed. It was revenge for what her father did to their kind."

"Do you kneow my father?" Elke said suddenly realizing what she most wanted to know. "Is he a guide now?" She wanted to think he was, that he could help them.

Nantan shook his head. "I cannot tell you all of what goes on-- especially that you could find for yourself," he said as he smiled and looked toward the canyon rim. "He is not a guide though."

"Reincarnated then?"

He shook his head. "Ask no more questions about what you can find for yourself when you need to know."

That sounded like all the spirit guides she'd ever known with their answering questions with questions or batting away hers as though she already had the answers. She knew one thing. If her father had not reincarnated and wasn't serving as a guide, it meant he had remained a ghost. He was free-acting and could be anywhere, doing anything. Instead of aiding others, he could be working for his own interests. What would those be? Once again, she thought how little she had known him.

"You believe I was manipulated into bringing her up here?" It was obvious Mitch didn't like that idea.

"Or fate." The old man shrugged. Fate was a term she'd heard often-- as an excuse for making no earthly sense.

"Do you believe Rugaru was after Elke?" Mitch asked, interrupting her train of thought. Nantan shrugged. "How do we keep her safe and get her out of here?"

"She could just dematerialize if she wishes. He's not so clever as to know she'd just be gone."

"And then keep killing any woman who comes along this trail," she said knowing that was not an acceptable option.

"Until Mitch is gone at least," Nantan agreed.

"And then he waits for more victims. We can't leave him here," Mitch said.

The old man shrugged. "Guess you don't want my advice this time either."

Mitch tightened his lips. "All right, I do need your advice."

"Rugaru does not know what we say. He is manipulated by the demon world, but they cannot hear what happens here. In that, you were wise to come here, grandson."

"I hoped to talk with you by coming here," Mitch admitted. "I never imagined I'd be putting Elke in danger. I thought I was keeping her safe."

"She was already targeted. She knew that-- didn't you, gal."

She nodded. "My family, and it's gotten more difficult."

Nantan chuckled. "Witches are often regarded as bad by my people, but some are good. Your family lives like Apaches with using magick only for good. Your father though… he's another story."

"You aren't suggesting my father is a bad man or ghost or whatever he is doing now?" She felt horrified at the very idea. It was not possible.

"Ain't I?" Nantan asked meeting her gaze without flinching. "I don't tell you what you want to hear but only what I believe is truth. Your father chose his own paths. I will say he believes it is for good. Despite that, he is drawing to his family the same sort of trouble as Mitch drew to himself through the foolish book."

"So what do we do now about this canyon and the one doing evil here?" Mitch asked. His eyes were troubled, his lips set in a grimace.

"You ready to listen now?" The old man's smile was mocking.

"If I was not, I'd not ask."

"Fine. So, don't run off. Leave Adolph and the horses here, where they are safe. Send Elke to the corpse. It will draw Rugaru. You go with her. Together, you defeat and destroy him."

"I like that idea," Elke said pleased at the way it felt.

"I don't," Mitch disagreed. "What if she is hurt?"

"And what if you are?" she argued.

"I started this."

She laughed at him. "You honestly believe that? If so, you have more ego than I thought."

She saw by the expression in his eyes that he didn't like that, but he didn't argue with her either. "So how do we proceed?" he asked turning back to his grandfather.

CHAPTER 12

"My suggestion is you wait for morning. Rugaru has already seen you there." He looked at Mitch. "He will be scenting her when she approaches."

"Why morning?"

"Time to prepare. The dark of the moon works in Rugaru's favor, not yours. Light benefits you unless you wish to go as a wolf."

"I need to use my sword. So human," Mitch said. Maybe his grandfather was right, and he didn't need him. He didn't feel that way.

"Other wolf shifters have killed them," Elke said.

"Perhaps they were more experienced in fighting as a wolf than I am."

"Let me go," Adolph requested with a wolfish grin.

"Not a chance. You guard the horses. Keep this canyon safe."

"I'll go as a human," Elke said, "unless you need me as a wolf."

"No, I think better human also," Nantan said. "Look innocent, as though out for a hike. If he's after you or even all women, he will be waiting. Rugarus are vicious hunters but stupid too."

"Good," she said and to his surprise, she looked almost eager.

"He's dangerous," Mitch reminded her.

She smiled at him and his grandfather. "Then I better get rest." She crawled into her tent.

"You will follow her? His grandfather asked.

"She did not invite me."

"She is good woman."

"I know."

The old man grinned. "Even if she is a witch."

"And a warrior."

"She's good as a wolf too," Adolph quipped. "If she'd just stay one, I'd take her for a mate."

"Thought that was how you were thinking," Mitch retorted.

"I'm not a dumb wolf." Adolph snickered.

"One more thing for you to think on, grandson, for when this is settled here."

"What?"

"Something made this canyon open territory for the demons to draw Rugaru to it. That means a human. You understand that."

Mitch considered his words. "I hear you."

"You will need to find that person before you go back to Tucson."

"And I am going back?" Mitch asked with a laugh. He knew he had to, but once again wondered at his grandfather. The old man claimed he didn't read minds, but how did he know so much?

"Just find the answer to that puzzle as to who betrayed you, or your land here will not be safe with you gone."

Mitch nodded. He lay on top his sleeping bag as Adolph curled alongside him. He didn't know where his grandfather slept, but he released the questions and problems to the night and slept better than he had expected. Light came before he expected it. He dressed in shorts and tennis shoes before he built up the fire and put on the coffee. His grandfather might've been around, but he didn't see him.

When Elke came out of the tent, she was in shorts and a tank top. Her hair was braided in a long queue on her back. He handed her a biscuit along with a cup of coffee. "You sure you want to do this?" he asked still concerned if this was safe for her, as he began breaking camp. When they finished with the monster, they'd have to head back to the ranch.

"Of course." Tying on tennis shoes, she gave him a bewitching smile that distracted him from what he should have been thinking. "The sooner the better."

"You take care of her," Adolph warned as Mitch belted his sword and sheathe to his waist. Mitch winked at him as he pulled out the sword to swing it a few times and loosen up. A few minutes later, he and Elke entered onto the mainstream.

"You will be careful," he said. "You told me you've never fought a monster."

"Is there something I should know?"

"Mostly not to take anything for granted. They may not be smart, but they are crafty. They didn't hang around this many centuries without having some tricks."

"You'll be there." She didn't seem as worried, as he thought she should be.

"But not close to you, where I will want to be. I don't like it but have no choice, or Granddad seems to think he won't come out."

"Rugaru doesn't have psychic powers?"

"It would appear not or not that great."

"You should drop back now. Aren't we getting close to her body?"

He reached for her and pulled her into a tight embrace as his lips descended and claimed hers. "Don't take any risks."

She smiled and brushed his jaw with her fingers. "I won't. You need a shave, did you know that?"

"When we get back to the ranch."

With that, she was gone, striding rapidly up the streambed acting as though she was on a recreational hike. He let her go ahead a bit but not so far he couldn't hear her walking. When she stopped, he assumed she was near the body. She let out a scream.

He saw the burst of energy as he ran forward, his sword out and ready to use. When he saw her, the beast was beyond and hunched down, now looking wary. When Rugaru saw Mitch, he tried to turn. Another energy bolt stopped him. Mitch lunged with the sword. As the monster turned, he shoved the sword into its body as it bit at him. His next stroke lopped off its head. In moments, it turned from a living form to a pile of ash and minerals.

"Is there only one?" Mitch asked as he looked around.

Elke had moved toward the ash pile. "It's all I saw." She looked around. "This is seriously weird. The body is gone."

Either the monster had consumed it, or something else had moved it. There would be nothing to report to the authorities. Poor woman. He wondered if her friends would tell anyone what they had seen. Or would they convince themselves, they'd seen nothing.

An unearthly shriek turned him toward it. There hadn't been just one. He saw Elke trying to turn and knew she'd not be in time. He threw himself between her and the charging Rugaru just as the claws came out and ripped his skin. His sword was upright, and he thrust it forward with all his might, felt it enter the beast, hewing it in two. As with the other, the energy changed, as it dissolved into a pile of ash, some kind of plasma, and glistening minerals.

Elke was at his side using her hands to close the gash the monster had opened on his shoulder. "I don't know if I can close this," she moaned, even as he felt her healing energy entering the wound. "It went deep," she whispered, sucking in breaths of air as she continued working over the bleeding cut.

The pain surged through his body. He rose, started to walk, and stumbled. Something was draining him. He sank to his knees. She put her mouth to the bleeding tear, and he felt her blowing energy into it. Her hands did not let go of holding the edges together. He'd been poisoned. Whatever was entering his body would kill him. Better him than her.

"Don't you dare give up on me," she snapped as she put even more energy into trying to heal the wound. Her face had paled.

"Go get Granddad, Adolph, and the horses."

"I can't leave you."

"You have to get them because I can't walk out of here. You sure as hell… can't carry me." He felt darkness coming over him, knew when she lowered him to the sandy beach and then he was alone—unless these two Rugarus weren't the only ones. He looked up at the canyon walls, heard the sound of the river moving past. Not a bad place to die.

Elke rematerialized in the canyon and saw by the worried expression on Adolph's face that he understood it wasn't good. "We have to get back to him," she said, quickly saddling the horses. She left their supplies where they were. Mitch could send Joe back for them. She looked up then and saw Nantan. "You must save him," she said as she mounted Pepper and led the other two.

"He will have to save himself," Nantan said. "It was always about him." With that, he was gone.

She wanted to scream but that wasn't going to help anyone. Fear surged through her. Maybe there'd been more than two. She had not expected the second one. Without Mitch's quick action, she'd have been the one on the beach maybe dying. He had saved her but at what cost. She put out energy waves to her mother as she headed Pepper down the canyon, with Adolph loping ahead, scenting out the way.

'What is wrong?' her mother sent back.

'Mitch has been hurt. A Rugaru got him with its claws before he killed it. It ripped a gash in his shoulder and… something more.'

'Poison?'

'That's what it acted like.'

'Give me all the details you can.'

She described the way he had slumped to the ground, how she had closed the wound, but left out that she had been the target. She'd tell her that later. 'We need magick.' She heard her mother's hesitation. 'You have to help him,' she argued.

'I will talk to my mother. She will know. Do what you can for now.'

'I am.' With that, she turned all her energy to getting back to Mitch and then him to the ranch. Could a doctor help with something like this? She had no idea what it might even be. Something more than a simple wound. Grandma Jess might be the only one to figure out what could counteract the poison.

When she got to Mitch, she was relieved he was still conscious and trying to hold the licking Adolph from getting at his face. She dropped to the beach to assess his condition.

"Ranger isn't spooking," he said as he raised himself to his elbows and watched the gelding who seemed perfectly calm. Given what had happened there, that was amazing.

"Can you get on Traveler?" she asked wondering if she could levitate him up.

"Sure." It took a little doing, but he made it into the saddle. He pointed to the rope. "Better tie me on just in case."

She gritted her teeth but by standing on a boulder, she managed it. Neither of them had any idea if this would get worse or if he had already experienced the worst of it. As they started to ride down the streambed, she said, "Mom is looking for antidotes."

"Good, I had no idea this could happen. Lucky in Mexico, I guess that… it ran off."

"They have mates," she said with her own shock. "So they reproduce."

He didn't respond to that, and she realized it was taking all the energy he had to stay on Traveler. She was proud of how Ranger was acting as he stayed with them, didn't tug on the lead line nor let Adolph running alongside frighten him. She kept looking over at Mitch, seeing how he slumped in the saddle, but he was still conscious. What could have been used on him? How would a Rugaru use such a thing? It had to have had help. Had it also had help in breeding? Cloning? Her mind went in useless circles as they climbed out of the canyon.

Once they got away from the water, the heat of the day was draining. She stopped Mitch's mount at intervals for him to drink, to make sure Adolph and the horses got water, and for herself. She didn't know how long it took. It seemed an eternity before she saw the ranch buildings.

When Joe Kuruk saw how they came riding up, he met them, helped to free Mitch from the ropes, and lowered him to the ground where he lay as though dead. Only his chest rising and falling told her he wasn't.

"What happened to him?" he asked looking up worriedly at her. His own face had paled.

"His shoulder was gouged," she said, wondering how much of Mitch's truth, his cousin knew. "It seems the animal's claws had been... poisoned."

Joe looked at the wound that although not bleeding still looked ugly. "Like no animal I seen..." He looked back up at her. "Heard of some though." His gaze was unwavering.

"Maybe that then... It's dead though." At least those two. Again, she decided to wait and let Mitch tell his cousin what he wanted him to know. She was surprised when Joe bent and picked up his cousin to carry him to the house. He hadn't seemed big enough to carry a man Mitch's size, but it appeared size wasn't everything. Adolph stayed at his heels.

At the door, Buck came out. "He doesn't look good," he said stating the obvious in Elke's mind.

"You take care of the horses," Joe told him and took Mitch up to his bedroom, laying him on the bed. "We need to get him cleaned up and assess this." He looked toward Sofia. "Call the doctor."

"No doctor," Mitch said with more strength to his voice than she'd expected. Apparently, concern of bringing in a doctor had roused him.

After that though, he lay without more protest and let Joe undress, wash him, and finally put him under covers. Adolph settled himself at the foot of the bed.

"So what we going to put on that wound?" Joe asked as he stepped back.

"I had a call into my mother, who knows about wounds," she said. "I'll check on what she's found." She went into her room and dug into her bag for her cell phone. Fortunately, it had held a charge.

"What did you find out?" she asked as soon as her mother picked up.

"Without a sample, can't know for sure, but the most likely Mom felt was hemlock. It's easiest to get and enough of it would kill a person. Through a bleeding wound though, it may have acted as a sedative—especially given his size. Get him coffee, any stimulant, and he'll probably be all right if the wound doesn't infect."

"It might. The Rugaru jumped out from the brush and used its claws." It was then she realized Joe had followed her. "Just a minute, Mom. Yes?" she asked, wondering how much he'd heard.

"He's asking for you."

"All right, in a minute. Mom says coffee, and I am guessing antiseptic cream, aloe, anything that fights infection and helps heal. Do you have poultices on hand? The way he keeps getting banged up, seems it might be wise to keep the herbs around." She smiled to soften her tough words. She was forcing away the fear that this could kill him. She would not let it.

He watched her for a moment before he turned to leave. "I'll tell Sofia."

"One more thing before you hang up," her mother said.

"All right."

"Something brought the Rugaru to the canyon."

"It might have been me." She told her then about the old spirit guide. "It was his opinion."

"Interesting… but still, it took someone on the earth level. Demons could bring up a Rugaru, but it would require an invitation. And one more thing." There was a silence. "Someone gave it the hemlock. A Rugaru would count on its claws and teeth being sufficient."

"A demon?"

"It still needs a human conduit."

"I'll think on it."

"Be careful and watch what is going on around there for who. Just as is happening here in Tucson, there may be more than one plotting."

Walking into Mitch's bedroom, his color already looked better. She bent and felt of his forehead. No fever. His eyes opened and looked lucid.

"Mom says it might have been hemlock, and if so, drink lots of coffee and stimulants of any sort."

He managed a laugh. "One comes to mind."

She sat on the edge of his bed and wagged her fingers at him "I doubt that's what she had in mind." Putting her hands over the wound, she let healing heat flow through her.

"Did she have... any thoughts on what we ran into?" He shifted with some discomfort. She let up until he seemed more at ease and then began again. The heat would hurt, but it would also heal.

"We didn't have long to talk." She plumped pillows behind him to ease him up for when the coffee arrived.

"Granddad?"

"He said you didn't need him."

"Enigmatic as usual. I guess we didn't."

She liked how he added the we. At that point, Joe came in with a tray and three mugs. "I didn't know if you took sugar or cream," he said as he put it on the dresser. "So, I brought both."

"Neither, thank you." She took the first cup to Mitch and helped him hold it as he sipped the hot brew.

"You going to tell me what actually went on up there?" Joe asked as he handed her a cup. Leaning against the dresser, he sipped his own, his gaze traveling from her to Mitch. She thought he looked uneasy, more than she'd have expected given Mitch appeared to be making a quick recovery.

"I think Mitch needs to rest for now," Elke said. She might have been overstepping her authority but wanted to talk to Mitch about Joe without him there.

Joe looked at her questioningly. When Mitch said nothing, he nodded and left.

"What's up?" Mitch asked.

"Does hemlock grow in your canyons here?"

"It's like Queen Anne's Lace but taller, right?"

"Yes and very poisonous."

"We tried to get rid of it all as it can kill cattle. Probably it'd still be on forest service land."

"My mother said not only did someone have to draw the monsters to the canyon but had to have told them about or given them the hemlock. Someone human. How much do you trust Joe?"

"Hmmmm. Let me think. He came to me... I guess four years ago. He is cousin to a cousin or something like that. He wanted work. He has been a good worker. He had questions especially about Apache mysticism, about magick-- even more after he read *Vislogus*. I taught him some simple techniques like meditation, not sorcery level though."

"Was he satisfied with that?"

"You think he went elsewhere for instruction?"

"He's in an area that he could do that if he had been so inclined."

"And find a bad source if he... Yeah, he could have."

"Is he inherently a good man?"

"I thought he was. Let me... think about that when my head is clearer."

"Well, don't trust him too much until you do."

He let out a breath but nodded. "I should get up."

She pressed back against his chest. "You should stay right where you are."

"You keep me entertained?" he asked with a teasing laugh. He definitely was feeling better.

"I might consider it when I stop worrying you might die." She did though lie down alongside him, putting her arm over his torso. "Energy exchanges like this will be good for you and me." She meant that, as she still felt shaky at what had almost happened. "You know," she added, "you saved my life."

"You might've turned in time to stop it."

"I don't think I could have. You put yourself between me and the attack and nearly got killed."

"I had the advantage of the sword."

She gave a little laugh. "Can't you just accept you are a hero?"

"I was no hero."

"I don't see how you can say that."

"I was scared that you'd be killed and more scared of that then what might happen to me. I didn't have time to think of anything to be honest."

"You can't escape it."

He gave a little laugh. "Escape what?"

"I belong to you now until I save your life anyway."

"Is this some kind of rule I haven't heard of?"

"Pinky swear."

He laughed again. "Now you really can't mean that."

"My grandma taught me." She took his hand and hooked her pinky over his. "This stands us good until I save your life."

He shook his head. Before he could say more, Joe came back into the room. Elke sat up and watched as he approached the bed.

"I wanted to know more about what happened out there,"

"Mitch is in no shape right now," Elke said. "He needs time to heal."

"Then when?" He looked edgy and to Elke's eyes guilty.

"Better we talk it out now," Mitch said. He adjusted the pillows at his back. Although she disapproved, Elke knew he might be right. Adolph had come to alert and was watching them.

"What do you know about Rugarus?" he asked Joe.

"Nothing… Oh wait, isn't there a kind of wolf god for some tribes. Not us though."

Elke looked at Mitch wondering what he was thinking as to her it was obvious Joe was lying and not doing a good job of it.

"Now tell me the truth," Mitch said, swinging his legs to the floor but keeping the sheet over his groin. "You keep lying, and I'll beat the hell out of you or give it a damned good try."

"Mitch," she said with her hand on his shoulder. "I could…"

He interrupted her. "No, this is my family. Now the truth, you bastard or so help me, you will regret it."

Joe looked away, tears ran down his cheek and then he slumped into the wooden chair. "All right… I… I thought I could surprise you and… get some magick that would… But then…"

"Damnit," Mitch interrupted. "Stop bawling and get the story out here before I let Elke kill you."

Joe looked uneasily at her. "She don't carry a gun."

"She doesn't need one."

"Oh." He looked at her more closely. "She like you then?"

"She's her own thing and has plenty to take care of you if you don't tell us the truth. And she's got a hogwash meter too. Lie to her, and she'll know."

Joe frowned. "All right..." He sighed and put his head in his hands before he looked up. "I went into Sedona for some books. You know that little shop where... Well, you know. And there was a man in the parking lot who came up to my truck as I got out. He said he was waiting for me. I said can't be. I didn't know I was coming. He said he knew.

"He put his arm around my back and led me over to the bench under the cottonwood where he told me I could learn magick, the kind my cousin had. See..." He turned and looked at Mitch. "He knew I had a cousin. That was meaning he was strong, right?"

"Go on," Mitch said his mouth tight but whether from pain or anger, Elke couldn't tell. Maybe some of both.

"Anyway, he drove me out to his house, and he said I'd learn what I needed there. He... well, he did teach me how to do things like bending a spoon."

"Parlor tricks," Mitch said with disgust.

"There was going to be more. He asked if I wanted more power to come to this land. Power that could make everybody like my cousin. Why should he have all the power? He said. I thought... I said yes. And then, he told me about monsters and how they can do good things, bring power back to my people that the white man took away. I mean, Mitch, you ain't all 'pache. Even you're half white. Why shouldn't a true blood brother have the power? I wanted it. I admit I wanted it and then..."

"It got away from you," Elke said.

"Yeah..."

"And the hemlock?"

"He told me to gather it but use gloves because it was powerful. He told me where to leave it. I didn't think. I... I was going to warn you when you rode out to the canyon, but then I thought... hell, nothing would happen. You have power." He sobbed. "Then I worried and when I saw you come back, looking dead, I knew I'd done wrong, but it was too late. Go ahead, kill me. I deserve it." He looked at Elke instead of Mitch.

"You don't have to die to start over. What you've taken as power can be taken from you, cleanse you of it," Elke said when Mitch said nothing.

"Then do it. I don't want it. I didn't handle it." He looked at Mitch who was staring at the ceiling. "I am sorry, cousin."

"Just... I need to rest," Mitch said letting out a breath as he slouched back down in his bed. His gaze met Elke's eyes. "I don't seem to know anything right now."

"It'll be clearer when you wake up." She kissed his forehead. Adolph indicated he'd stay with him, and Elke followed Joe out onto the lower patio where they would have privacy.

"You can really clear away the stuff I did?" Joe asked as he turned and watched her.

"Do you understand all you did?"

"I nearly got Mitch killed, didn't I?"

"Or me."

"You?"

"I may have been the intended target."

He put his hands over his face. "I am so sorry."

"Where did you put the hemlock?"

"On a little island in the canyon."

"All of it?"

"Yes."

"What you did could have gotten you killed also."

"I wish I'd never gotten jealous, wanted what Mitch had. I am sorry."

She let her powers enter his mind and search for the truth. When she decided he had held nothing back. "Do you truly wish the magick to be gone? All that you saw as power to be forgotten?"

He nodded. "More than you'll ever know. I was a fool to believe that man. I hate it. Stuff kept happening, and I didn't know how to stop it. It sucked me into it."

She smiled at that. It sounded very like a young boy, which was about how Joe was looking after his emotional storm. "So, Joe, how do you feel about witches?"

He clenched his jaw, looking some like Mitch when he did it. "Ain't met one yet... Okay, you're saying I have."

"I am saying that, and because of what I have been taught, down through the rules and order of the people who have long taught a right use of magick, I can clear you. Not of all you know but of all the falsehoods you were given. You will have to start over where it comes to magick-- if you should ever so wish to follow that path again."

"Only if it's with Mitch. Clear me if you can."

"Lie on the ground." She circled around him and began to chant the words she'd long ago been taught-- the ones that gave all power over to the light, and all goodness had to come from it. Although she knew the meaning of the words, she liked using the old language.

It took maybe an hour although she lost track of time between the chants and songs, that pulled her into a different place, intensified her aura and with it all, drew to her the powers of the Elementals as they agreed and lent their own energy to the task.

"In harmony with the Universe, and the One, I declare this man cleansed of ill intent and purposes. And so be it."

She moved from him to sit on one of the lawn chairs and watch him come back to himself. The look in his eyes had changed. When he sat up, he looked at her. "Thank you," he said. "I do feel different."

"If they try to contact you, use these words." She gave him a simple affirmation that he could remember. "Repeat three times and they will have to go. Right now is not a good time for you to again attempt to take on magick, not even with Mitch, but he will know when the time comes."

"You think he'll ever forgive me?"

"You've known him longer than me. Do you think he's the type to hold a grudge?"

Joe managed a weak smile and shook his head. "No, he's not."

"Go rest now."

Time fell away from her as night fell over the beautiful valley, a soft, comforting darkness with stars twinkling overhead. All around felt good and at peace. She had one more task to complete as she sent out energy to the place the Rugaru had been and where the hemlock had been left. When she recognized its vibrations, she used a power blast to annihilate it, avoiding the chance of someone else accidentally coming across it. She sensed no more Rugarus in the area but that didn't mean some would not arrive.

She thought then of the body of the murdered girl, the one someone might have thought was her. She asked for mercy for her soul and peace. Maybe it had been the girl's time, but it made Elke feel sad and a little guilty that someone innocent might have died in the place of her.

Sitting in one of the lawn chairs, Elke had never known anything like she felt here in this house and on this land. As much as she had loved Tucson, something here was agrarian and serene. She knew there were evil spirits nearby, ghosts who should have gone on, maybe even her father was one, but this place could be kept safe. The question was—could Tucson? She had to go back and do what she could to make that happen—no matter what the cost. No more innocent lives must be lost.

CHAPTER 13

When Mitch woke at first light, he felt sore but stronger. He was surprised to find Elke sleeping alongside him. He lay watching her. Her lashes were dark against her cheek. When her eyes were open, they were so expressive, even fiery. Those beautiful eyes drew him to them more even than the rest of her features like the high cheekbones, the full, very kissable lips. He contemplated kissing her awake when he realized she was now watching him.

"How do you feel?" she asked, reaching to touch his forehead.

"Better." He didn't need to add as though a mule had kicked him. He was lucky to be alive, and he knew it. Two run-ins with the monsters should be a limit but then he wondered about the old saying about things running in threes.

"Quit worrying," she ordered, brushing his lips with her fingertips.

"I blame myself for this whole thing. I should have seen what was happening with Joe."

"Ah, omnipotent now, huh?" she suggested with a little laugh. She got up and headed for the shower. He heard the water running, knew he needed one too, but if he went in, it'd not be a shower he'd be taking. They needed to talk about that too. He had told himself they had no future. He wondered if she agreed with that. He wanted her to argue him into why they could have one. What a weakling.

When she came out, he went in and stood under the hot water, sudsing his body, and trying not to imagine her drying off her soft skin and then sliding into her clothing. He was too far gone to kid himself that he he didn't want her and for more than a day. He kept coming back to that not being logical. They had nothing in common. Probably would fight all the time. She would draw as many enemies to her as he did. What a team... but then again, what a team.

When he came out of the shower, he dressed in shorts and a t-shirt as she watched. "You know we both should have been more aware of Joe, me more than you," she said as he came to sit beside her on the bed.

"He isn't your cousin."

"But I'd seen how this worked before. Nick Beringer had a step-brother, who Ornis used. Someone near is who we most should watch for changes. When a stepbrother or in your case, a cousin, wants to be you, then they are vulnerable. We can't afford to forget that again."

"Again?" He reached out and took her hand, stroking her fingers.

"Your want to be stepbrother is one."

"Him I wouldn't ever trust."

"This is a war, Mitch. The other side uses all they can find against us. You knew that in *Vislogus*, and after meeting you, I understand it better also. I suppose like all wars, there will be a truce at some point, or we will get a better understanding of what is behind it, but for now, we can't afford to relax."

"And what comes next?"

"I have to go back to Barrio Viejo. I think the battle there is just beginning. I have to be with my family, as it will take all we have. I fear it could be more than we have. It's being fought on several levels. So far, no monsters there, at least not that I knew, but human and demonic powers. A woman was killed and that has to be resolved. A church, led by a man who is not operating under the One, is at war with my family—at war with all that is good."

"All right."

She smiled and brushed her fingers over his lips. "You need to shave while I go see what Sofia has figured out for breakfast. I smell coffee."

He rubbed his hand over his bristle. "Is there any special reason I need to shave?"

She laughed and ran out of the room.

When he entered the kitchen, Sofia looked up with surprise. "I thought you'd be in bed today. I was readying a tray."

"I'm mostly just tired now." He sat at the table, across from Elke. "When do you need to leave?" he asked.

"I am not in a hurry. I'd like us to discuss a plan."

"You're going to listen to me?" he asked with more than a little surprise.

"How about if we eat breakfast on your beautiful patio," she suggested, rather than answering his question. "I love the morning outside."

"What would you like?" Sofia asked.

"Scrambled eggs, toast for me," Mitch said. "Can you bring it out there?" When she agreed, he followed Elke to sit at the table in the sun, feeling it energizing him.

"You look much better today."

"I feel better. Just tired. As for a plan, I'd like to go with you when you go, but I am not up to much yet."

"It would be safer for you to stay here. Whatever is going wrong in Tucson will involve human evil. I almost think I'd prefer monsters. You can kill them with a sword and the bodies disappear with no questions from police to answer." She gave a little laugh.

Sofia came out with a tray heaped with eggs, bacon, toast, jam, butter, a coffee pot, and cut up fruit. Elke waited for Mitch to fill his plate, then filled her own mostly with the fruit and a piece of toast, snatching a piece of bacon to munch.

"As for a plan, you are looking for a murderer in Tucson," he said as he ate. "One who now has killed three women."

She shook her head. "No, I told you. This is a different murderer, someone who wanted to hide his murder behind the fear it's a serial killer."

"You told me that before. Now tell me how you know."

"My family and I knew that it was a man called Braddock, who had ties to both women. He operated as a sorcerer in Tucson— someone others went to for instruction with great spiritual wisdom." She laughed with no humor. "Like the man, who contacted your cousin, he was playing with the dark side. In the end, we drained him of his power."

Mitch let out a whistle. "Like you did Joe?"

She shook her head. "There are levels. I truly believe Joe didn't mean wrong. He got another chance. Braddock knew exactly what he was doing. He's a shadow man, who preys on the vulnerable and went beyond it when he murdered with an intent of framing Nick."

"You could have killed him. Why not?"

She shrugged. "Maybe it was a mistake but it seemed more just. Instead of just taking the magick he'd acquired, we also drained his fleshly energy to leave him alive but no longer capable of plotting or doing more than surviving. Maybe it was more cruel. The thing is that the law would have never dealt with him. He didn't leave evidence, and black magick is not something a court system would recognize. Sometimes those with spiritual power have to mete out justice—when it can't be done any other way."

"You and your family became judge, jury and stopped short of executioner." He wasn't sure how he felt about that. His own battle with the spirit world had not been against humans. Even having human enemies, his father's ex-wife and her son, he'd never thought of using his otherworldly power to resolve that situation.

"I guess you could say that," she said accurately reading his concern. "We had spirit guides and an angel along with us. I won't claim we asked for a Divine edict. Should we have left him to kill again? Ornis was helping him, and you know what he does."

He did know that. It still bothered him.

"Do you want me to go?" she asked her gaze levelly on him.

"It's too late for that." He shook his head with a twisted smile.

"Of course, it's not. I would go if you asked."

"I don't ever want you to go, but I've learned the hard way though in life, that what I want is not always how it is going to be."

"I'm used to getting what I want," she said, rising and coming around the table. "Are you up to a woman on your lap?"

He pulled her down, stretching her long legs across his, and putting his arms around her. "It would depend on the woman." She bent then and kissed him lightly before he turned the kiss into something headier by thrusting his tongue into her mouth as she met him with her own teasing touches.

When she pulled her head back, she said, "You and I are different."

"I know." He liked the feel of her on his lap.

"I want you to meet my family. They are a little crazy."

"Crazier than you?"

"Different. Maybe Grandma Elsa is a little more." She giggled.

"You all meet to have planning sessions then?" She nodded. "Do they have to okay me?"

Before she could answer, Joe came up from the barns. He looked sheepish. "Do you want me to leave?" he asked Mitch without sitting down.

"Want some of Sofia's breakfast?" Mitch asked pointing to all the food left on the table.

"You willing for me to eat at your table?"

"Sure."

"I could have cost you... or her your lives."

"You're smarter now though, aren't you?"

Joe's laugh was a little sick sounding. "I sure hope so."

"Go beyond hope. Be sure of it."

Joe nodded. "Then I'm not fired?"

"Nope. You're a good man with horses. I need you. Now that you know more, you should be a bigger help."

Joe let out a sigh. "I am sorry."

"I know. So eat already."

∾

An hour later, Elke had talked to her mother and decided there was no rush to get back to Tucson. She wanted more time with Mitch, wanted him to be fully back to health. The truth was she didn't want to leave this place, but she had no choice—eventually.

"Want to see the vineyard?" he asked as he came out from the house dressed in jeans, a light cotton shirt, and the usual boots.

"I'd love to. When do you harvest the grapes?"

"When Jacque says. He just called, and he'll be down there to assess the timing. I thought you might like to meet him."

"I'd love that." A few minutes later, they were at the edge of what seemed miles of grapes on wooden supports. "It's beautiful," she said. "I've never actually been in a vineyard."

"Ours have several varieties; so the harvesting times vary." He picked a grape from the vine and popped it into her mouth and then another for himself.

"Sweet," she said. "Are these grapes all for sweet wines?"

"Nope, that's determined by how long they ferment. The same grapes can make dry or sweet." He bent and claimed her lips with a

151

kiss. "There is a kind of sensual element to making wine. Did you know that?"

She laughed. "About all I know regarding wines is to order white or red and leave it up to the waitperson as to which is best with my dinner."

He brushed his finger lightly over her lips and cupped her chin so that she looked into his eyes. "Well there is the picking, of course..." He drew her into his arms.

"Do you do that mechanically?" she asked leaning into him.

"No, it has to be by hand. Jacques says it's much better for the grapes that way." He ran his hands down her back to cup her buttocks, pulling her more tightly against his groin. She felt his hardness, and it stirred her body.

"And then?"

"There is the press... Unfortunately, these days we don't do that with bare feet... A pity, but evidently mechanically is better and more sanitary."

"I can't even imagine what it must have felt like to wade through grapes."

"Maybe we can do a small batch sometime." He laughed and brushed his lips over her forehead. A truck, coming in the drive and stopping, interrupted whatever play he might've considered next. Just thinking what it might've been stirred her senses.

A dark-haired, middle-aged man got out of the truck and walked over to shake Mitch's hand and be introduced to Elke. "You are a genius at wines, I am told," she said.

"Mitch is too kind," Jacque said. He had no accent but had a Mediterranean look to his skin and features.

"It was actually my sister, Torre. She's the wine connoisseur. I am a novice at it. When we eat out, I let her pick the wine. To be honest, my total skill is recognizing one that is corked." She gave a little laugh. "And I am not being modest."

Jacques grinned. "Then you can learn if you have a good teacher." He smiled at Mitch.

"I am just learning too," Mitch said. "I am, however, appreciative of your skills."

"After they are pressed, without bare feet," Elke said, "what happens next?"

Jacques picked a grape and ate it. "You will see that soon if you are here. Perhaps in a week for the first."

"How exciting."

"Mitch always is here for the harvest... or has been. Will you be this time, *amico*?" Jacques asked.

"I have to go to Tucson on business, but I'll be back if it's in a week."

"Good." He turned back to Elke. "As to what comes next, well, they aren't all ready at the same time—fortunately." He looked affectionately at the grapes as though they were his children. "After the pressing, we produce what is called must. That is when we remove the skins, seeds and solids for the white wines. Reds and whites each go into their own big oak barrels for fermenting, which varies for how long-- depending on sweet or dry.

"After that, any solids are removed, and they can be put into bottles or back into oak barrels to age—depending on the quality of the harvest. A fine wine might set in the barrels for two years. It is all done by the touch." He grinned. "Like touching a beautiful lady. It must be just right and then... voila, they are bottled and sent to buyers or sometimes to competitions. Nothing like many ribbons to up the price." He chuckled changing his sensual words into practical ones.

As they talked and walked through the vineyard, alive with bird, butterflies, and bees, Elke's body and mind were astir with energy and desire. Mitch's hand rested lightly at her waist, very innocent gesture, but she found herself imagining it other places. She wanted to touch him again, stroke his strong body, make love to him, while he made love to her. When she looked up into his eyes, she krew he was feeling the same things.

"Thanks for the lessons and tour, Jacques," Mitch said as they walked him back to his truck. After waving good-bye, Mitch turned back to her. "The river is beautiful this time of the year. Want to see it?"

"I'd love to."

"I'll get us a quilt." His smile told her what he had in mind. Half an hour later, he had a quilt and basket, and they were standing beside the Verde. Big cottonwoods and willows shaded its grassy banks. Because there hadn't been many strong storms, the water was not bank full, more a sleepy river. He spread the blanket and lowered himself to look up at her. "Is white all right?" he asked.

"Lovely." She sat beside him and watched the river as she heard him opening the bottle, then pouring the wine. He handed her a plastic cup. They sipped without words. She wanted to make love with him, but she also found her mind going again and again to a murderer in Tucson. Some romantic partner she was.

"Are you having doubts about us?" he asked.

She looked at him. "No, not at all. More just concerned about what happened in Tucson."

"The murder or the religious fanatics?" She was surprised he was so willing to redirect his own thoughts from what she knew he'd been planning.

"The murderer. The fanatics will always be with us."

"Okay, you won't enjoy what I had in mind until we talk about it. Tell me again what you know."

"The only thing I hadn't mentioned was that when I went out to the site with Detective Myers, where they found the body, I sought a vision. Sometimes I can do that, you know feel what happened somewhere. I had no feeling that a murder happened there. What I saw was a heavyset man carrying and then positioning the body before walking away. I never saw his face."

"Interesting." He sipped his wine as he stared at the river. "What was his energy?"

"Angry and rushed."

"Violent?"

She considered that. "I didn't get that. More upset. The feeling I have is it was Pastor Jefferies, but since I didn't see a face, I can't say for sure it was him. He'd have had no reason to be there, but Debbie did work for him until he said he had fired her the day before."

"When you were with him, did you get murderer vibes?"

"I was blocked and that was strange. I disliked him so much that… it's hard to be objective, but no, I didn't. Abuser maybe but not a murderer."

"Okay, let's think of reasons why he might've been there with the body."

"What do you mean?"

"Maybe he was only about body disposal. If the murderer was someone else, then, who would he want to protect, to take the risk of being with a body? And, even at night, he could have been seen. Then, there is how he positioned it, in the crucified pose was that sick or purposeful in terms of a religious mentality—or trying to get revenge on someone he thought it might finger?"

"Are you a writer?" she asked teasingly, reaching out to stroke his cheek.

"In the five years I was near my father, lots of plots were always being thrown at him."

"What about the man whose arm you broke."

"Definitely he had something untoward in mind, but would a murderer strike again so quickly after killing one person? Did you get an autopsy report on the girl?"

"No, it hadn't been in before you kidnapped me."

He laughed. "Don't use that word around your detective friend. I might end up the one in jail."

"Since I am only planning to tease you with it, you are safe." She giggled. "I should call Mom or Torre to see if they have determined cause and time of death."

"Good idea." He put down his wine glass and leaned her back on the blanket. "And now for more important business."

"And what would that be?" she asked as he began to kiss his way down her cheek to her neck."

"Think on it. It'll come to you."

An hour later or maybe more, she came back to reality as she thought about how Mitch stroked all her right spots and that included intellectually as well as physically. She watched him, his eyes closed. "What are you thinking?" he asked.

"Nothing," she lied.

He laughed and looked up at her. "I know what I'm thinking. You are everything I want in a woman. I want to be all you want in a man."

"We haven't known each other long," she reminded him-- or maybe it was herself.

"Does that matter?"

"You might find you don't much like the idea of a witch for a... friend."

"Friend was not what I had in mind. I want you as a mate... and since you are a witch, then I guess I want a witch."

"It can get difficult."

"Like I am easy to get along with."

"Are you warning me?"

"Some. I don't know where we're going with this, but I want us to move forward."

She considered that. "You really want to drive back to Tucson with me?"

"No."

She understood that. "I think I can do this without you."

He snorted. "I don't doubt that but that's not what I have in mind. I feel good enough now. I'll fly us down. I have a Citation CJ3. Are you familiar with it?"

She came from a rich family but not that rich. "No."

"It's reliable, fast, and we can be down there whenever you want… and back here by night—if we want."

It was her turn to laugh. "You are a pilot."

"I am and a good one."

"Do you commute then?"

"I hadn't but could if I had a reason. I think we should both stay at your place though… if that's okay with you."

She hadn't expected that. "Why?"

"Somebody tried to break into your home. It seems to me that person could be back… with a cast and sling." His smile was crooked. "I am sure you could take care of them, but I want to be there too. Maybe we can… uh convince the man to tell us what he knows about Debbie's murder."

"That seems a longshot."

"We'll see. Besides you're closer to good restaurants, and I don't intend to bring Sofia."

"You doubt I can cook?" she teased grabbing a long grass stem and teasing his lips with it.

"With everything else in your package… pretty much, yeah." He leaned over, and she forgot the rest of what she was thinking.

When they went back to the house, she called her mother to see what was happening. When it was nothing new, they decided to fly down early in the morning to beat a promised thunderstorm. In the evening, he suggested they watch a DVD. He had one room with a huge screen

TV and hundreds of DVDs. "How do I pick from all of these?" she asked as she looked at a bookcase almost the length of a wall.

"Some were my father's collection, and I had them made into DVDs when that became an option. He had all his films, but many of the ones of his friends and even enemies." He laughed. "I still get sent DVDs of new films by directors he worked with or those who remember him. Maybe hoping I'll review them. Good and bad, I have a lot of what's ever been made."

Finally, she chose one she'd seen many times, but it never got old, *Casablanca*. They settled onto a long sofa. Sofia brought them popcorn before she headed for bed.

"This is a wonderful place," Elke said, as she wiped away the tears from the ending. Something she always had to do.

"It's a sanctuary for me. I don't live here year round but maybe should."

"You aren't fond of people?"

"I can be with them when it's required. The reason I avoided publicity after the book came out is the whole Paparazzi thing. With my father being who he was, my wantabe stepmother being who she is, I knew not being known was safer and made my life more peaceful."

"And your stepbrother?"

"Who actually never was since he wasn't my father's son. I see him when he needs money. That's about it. Except the stupid article he sold."

"I did read that." She felt herself flush. "I was stalking you."

He chuckled. "And now I'll help you do it. Stalk me all you want."

"I was half in love with Adolfo."

"Better mate for you would be Adolph," the wolf said before he put his head back down.

Elke laughed, not sure Mitch found it so humorous. She brushed his tawny hair back behind his ear.

"One thing hasn't changed," Mitch said. "I won't let you use the book for a play."

She suppressed her feeling of annoyance. "Did you think that's what this was about?"

"No. You're not that kind of woman. Just saying."

"Well, you can say all you want. Maybe I can write my own play now based on what happened in the canyon. It's not like you own that."

"Why don't we argue this out-- after you get your murderer nailed."

"Was that a plotted distraction?"

"Maybe." He laughed. "I am coming to know you well enough to know some possible ways to do that."

"Two can fight that way." She put her fingers out to brush over his chest where the vee in his shirt opened.

"Fight that way all you want, baby. That kind of distraction works for me."

"Me too."

"Am I going south with you?" Adolph asked lifting his head again.

"Not this time. I want you here to keep an eye on the ranch."

"You think it'll be dangerous for me," the wolf argued.

"Or that you'll go after my woman."

Adolph chuckled but didn't argue further.

"Am I your woman?" she asked liking the sound of that.

"If you want to be."

"There are things to work out."

"We can do that... if you want to."

She wanted to. She just wasn't sure it was possible—assuming he even stayed alive. He seemed to have a tendency to court danger.

CHAPTER 14

The flight south from the Verde Valley on Mitch's plane was smoother than Elke had been expecting given the promised storm in the afternoon. He handled the plane with ease and soon they were landing at Tucson International where he taxied into a hangar.

"I don't want it beat to death with hail today," he said as they grabbed their bags, disembarked, and he left the plane in the care of one of the uniformed tenders. "Fuel it up," he directed, "and give it a once over to be sure everything is in shape for when I need it."

The man smiled. "No problem, Mitch. Give us a call, and we'll get it out when you want it."

She was surprised that an SUV was also waiting for him. The privileges of his level of wealth went beyond anything she'd imagined. For the first time, she began to wonder exactly how much money he had. Wealth could be a barrier she had not imagined.

"You hungry?" he asked, as they drove out of the parking garage.

"Could we stop by a grocery store, and I'll get some food for back at my apartment."

"You sure?" He raised his brows with skepticism.

"Nothing complicated. Just bread, sliced turkey, roast beef, horse-radish, lettuce, eggs, bacon, some basics like wine and beer."

He grinned and pulled the SUV into the grocery parking lot. She expected him to wait in the vehicle, but he followed her in.

She had already figured that Mitch was the kind of man who could not walk anywhere without being seen just for his unusual height and that lion's mane of his. Then there was his resemblance to his movie star father, whose movies were still on the old movie channels as well as available as DVDs. Doubtless, some staring wondered why he looked familiar. Whatever it was, heads turned as he passed. Although Elke knew herself to be an attractive woman, she'd never had that kind of attention, walking alongside what amounted to a celebrity. She wondered if he was aware of the notice he drew. Probably so, and it's why he had been so reclusive.

"You like chocolate or vanilla ice cream?" he asked as he looked in the frozen food section.

"Cookies and cream," she said.

He put one of those and another flavor she'd never seen. So, he was an ice cream person. Another of those things she hadn't known. When Pepsi went into the cart, she learned something more.

"How about for breakfast?" she asked as she threw a sack of Seattle's Best coffee beans into the cart.

"Anything except dry cereal," he said. In the fruit section, he added a bag of small oranges to her apples. "You have any potatoes?" he asked studying the varieties.

"Carbs," she protested.

He laughed and put a 5 lb. sack of Goldens alongside the fruit. She headed back to the meat counter to add a package of chicken breasts. Mitch threw in a flatiron steak. Butter, cheese, and bread were also not the usual for her, but then nothing about this was the usual. She realized given his size, he probably took in a lot of food. She'd need to do much jogging, if she didn't want her hips to explode along with this relationship.

By the time, they got to the cash register, the cart was a lot fuller than she'd expected. Before she could get out her credit cards, Mitch had pulled out a roll of hundreds and paid cash. At the SUV, he stowed the groceries, and she returned the cart.

When he turned the SUV back onto the street, she said, "So there are multiple reasons why you avoid people."

He gave a little laugh. "Yeah, you get used to it in a way. In another way, you never do."

"I suppose being with your father, you saw that a lot, especially where you look like a younger version of him."

"Some. Do I turn here?" he asked. "I was only there once and came in from the other side."

"The next road."

"As for my father, I am taller than he was. I would guess if he'd been my height, he'd have not had the career he did. Dwarf all his leading ladies. I get called giant a lot." He looked over at her. "Lucky you're a tall woman."

"I've always liked being able to see over the crowds."

"There is that... After we unload the groceries, I'll park a few blocks from your place."

"You really are hoping to set a trap?"

"It's possible. If not, we'll have to do more detective work, check to see if hospitals let us know if that night they set a broken arm. I am hoping we get him the easy way when he shows up again."

Having a potential murderer show up in her apartment was the easy way? She tried to divert herself from her worries of how many ways this could go wrong—especially if the killer had a weapon.

"When will you be willing to meet my family?" She wasn't sure how that would go. Her mother would instantly be hearing wedding bells. Her grandmothers would be suspicious of his spiritual powers-- well, Grandma Elsa might do some lusting. Her unmarried sisters would be watching him with their tongues hanging out-- slight and only slight exaggeration.

"Let's talk about that when I get back." He helped her carry up their bags and groceries before driving off while she put everything away. It would seem strange to have him in her home. It was then that she heard the crash of thunder and flare of a lightning bolt. Moments later, he was running up the stairs. "It let loose," he said as he came in the apartment shaking his head and throwing water drops. She handed him a towel.

Drying his hair, he walked into her living room and opened the door to the deck. "This is nice," he said, watching as the rain pummeled the bougainvillea, bushes and trees.

"We needed this kind of storm," she agreed.

"Your place is nice."

"Thank you. Not very big by your standards."

"Big enough for now." He smiled. "I guess you'd want to live in the barrio if you were married or something."

"I have liked it here but not as well as your ranch... if you are

hinting at where would we live if we were trying to put a life together
—which I know you haven't asked to do."

"You've felt secure here, but I notice you don't have a very good
lock on your door."

"I never felt it was a problem."

"Those energy bolts can't protect you from everything."

"Well, there might be a few other things." She smiled and headed
back into the kitchen, returning with two beers. "I didn't ask if you
wanted one."

"I do."

"I can fix a sandwich," she said as a lightning flashed and the crash
was almost immediate. "Or if you like, I do know how to fix fettuccini.
It's pretty easy—if we don't lose power anyway."

"Sandwich now. Fettuccini later," he said with a smile, "and I can
put together my own sandwich." They went into the kitchen and came
back to eat on the covered deck, and watch the storm as it moved up
the valley. Nature's electrical storm surged all around them. When the
thunder crashed overhead, it was hard not to jump, but being with
him, his arm around her, helped.

"I should call Mom, I guess," she said, when the thunderstorm had
mostly passed. She knew her mother would already know she
was back.

"Want me to go outside while you talk?" he asked.

"Not needed. She will know you're here, and you and I have no
secrets." She hoped anyway.

"Hi sweetie," her mom said when she picked up.

"Have you all figured out the murderer yet?" she asked going right
to the point. She liked watching Mitch as he sat back on her sofa, his
attention on the sky as the clouds changed colors in the aftermath of
the storm.

"No, can you come tomorrow and we'll put our collective heads
and magick together."

"Sure. What time?"

"Say eleven and you can have lunch." There was a brief silence.
"Mitch is with you, isn't he?"

"Yes, he flew me down."

"Bring him, and I'll suggest Denali bring Nick. We can use some
masculine thinking."

"Sounds good. See you then."

"You're invited, and Nick will be there too," she said when she sat beside Mitch. "Did you ever meet him?"

"Nope. I bought his work from Jane Elm."

"They will grill you."

He chuckled. "About murders or you?"

"Both."

"I am up to it." He put her hand on his growing hardness. "Among other things."

"I like that 'other things'."

In the morning, they had a relaxed breakfast, which he fixed since he was more gifted at scrambled eggs than she was. Sipping their coffee on the deck, Elke saw Maya coming out to survey the damage to her garden. She hollered down to her and introduced her to Mitch.

"You look like you got some strength in this one," Maya said teasingly.

"This one? It's not like I've had that many men here," Elke protested.

Maya giggled. "The muscular sort are handy."

"Did you need help with something?" Mitch asked.

"The wind broke off the top of my pepper tree. I guess I should have trimmed it back anyway. I am not good with a saw though."

Mitch smiled. "Be right down."

While he was gone, Elke called Torre. "Will you be there today?" she asked her sleepy sounding sister.

"I hadn't planned on it."

"Mitch Ford will be there."

"I could change my mind."

Elke laughed. "Would you do me a favor and see if you can find hospital or ER admittance records for the 23rd or 24th and a male seeking treatment for possibly a broken arm?"

"I'll see what I can do. You know hospitals aren't so open about patient records."

"I know. That's why I wanted a hacker."

"I'll see what I can do." She heard the smile in Torre's voice. "Is he old and wizened or cute?"

"In a few hours, you can decide that for yourself."

An hour later, after Mitch had done more than a few favors for

Maya and earned her effusive gratitude, he was back upstairs. "I will need a shower before I meet your family," he said.

She thought he looked very enticing, sweat and all, but she nodded. They didn't have time for her to join him, but that idea was inviting also. He was proving to be very addictive.

When Mitch parked the SUV where Elke directed, he saw an assortment of vehicles already in front of the large house. "I grew up here," she said. "Never lived anywhere else until I got my apartment, but I suppose you knew that," she said as they walked up the sidewalk, past the gate, to the house.

"I did." Many things had changed for him in meeting the man who would become his mentor in warfare. He wondered what his life would have been like had that never happened. Useless pondering, of course.

"Wow, he's a big one," a white-haired lady said as she popped off a living room sofa.

"Be nice," Elke said. "Ladies and others, this is Mitchell Ford."

Maria rose and gave him a hug. "This one and I met before but just casually. I doubt you remember me."

"Oh I remember the beautiful lady at the meeting to discuss options for the homeless," he said with a smile as he got all the other names. "These ladies are way too young to be your grandmothers," he said as Elsa and Jess rose and gave him welcoming hugs.

"He's a keeper," Elsa said. She gave her granddaughter a look. "Don't let him get away."

"I am doing my best," Elke said with a laugh.

"I'm Nick," a tall, black-haired man said coming in from the kitchen with a cup of coffee in his left hand and taking Mitch's hand with his right. "Denali's other half." A gorgeous blonde, carrying a tray of pastries, was behind him and also shook Mitch's hand.

"Tea and coffee in the kitchen," Maria said. "We will then convene our meeting."

"I'm fine," he said sitting in a large overstuffed chair. Elke sat on its arm.

"To start," Torre said, "I have yet to find anything on a broken arm being set. I haven't given up though."

"Explain all this to us," Maria asked Elke, who then described the night someone had tried to break into her home and how Mitch had dealt with it.

Jess nodded approvingly. "As the wretch deserved."

"How much do you remember of what the man looked like," Maria asked.

"It was dark, no moon, no streetlights. It all happened fast. He was shorter than me."

Devi giggled. "But then almost everybody is, aren't they?" Then she flushed. "I didn't mean to insult you."

"You didn't. I am trying to remember. His features were nothing that stood out."

"Take us through the event," Denali suggested. "Maybe as you remember it, we will get something."

"You know that person might not be the killer," Jess said adding a note of practicality.

"It was someone though who had bad intentions," Elsa argued.

"Of course," Jess snapped back.

"All right," Mitch said hoping to smooth the waters. "I came up to the house intending to... talk to Elke. I saw the guy, realized he had a knife, and he went straight to the lower gate with it ready to jimmy the lock. When I broke his arm, he dropped the knife. After he ran off, I kicked it into the oleander before I opened the lock and went upstairs. That means it's probably still there with his fingerprints. I don't think he was wearing gloves."

Torre looked the most interested he'd yet seen. "I will see if it's still there. I have gloves to handle it. We can get the fingerprints or should we tell the police and let them get it?"

"Who would be in trouble then?" Mitch asked. "I did break his arm."

"A man intending to break into Elke's apartment," Maria said. "Maybe a man who is into assaulting and murdering women."

"If it wasn't random, then it had to be connected to the theater or church," Elke said. "Chuck had already gotten aggressive with me and come around when he wasn't welcome. From the way she had reacted that night, I would say Debbie and he had some connection where she felt betrayed." She described that event at Stage Left.

Torre reached into her purse and clicked on her iPad. "What's his name?"

"Chuck or maybe Charles Carter. He's been in several local productions. Action hero type... supposedly."

After some swiping, Torre turned the screen so Mitch could see it. "Look familiar?"

"It was dark but... what height is he?"

Torre swiped again. "Six foot... which means probably 5'10" as they always lie." She giggled.

"It could be him. Wish I'd broken his neck now," Mitch said with a low growl.

Nick laughed. "Disposing of bodies isn't easy-- in case you didn't know."

Mitch shook his head. What kind of family was he entering into? Well, given his own background, it was probably the perfect one—at least for him. Feeling Elke's warmth next to his side, he knew it was more than perfect.

"I'll see if I can find whether that person showed up at an ER," Torre said.

"Wouldn't he have to?" Devi asked.

"Was it a compound break?" Torre asked as she kept punching in keys.

"It could have been. I slammed him hard," Mitch said. "He was holding it as he ran off."

"If it was," Denali said, "if he didn't go to the doctor, he had to have someone help him. Elke, any idea who his friends are?" She was cuddled against Nick in what seemed a natural and loving way. If once, Mitch had been cynical about relationships, he now wanted to see them as possible. The truth was it was too late for him to walk away from Elke. He had to go forward with this—for whatever was possible.

"I don't know him, other than he's uncouth and was drunk the first and probably at least drinking the second time I saw him."

"So might whatever he had going with Debbie have given him enough reason to kill her?"

Elke shook her head. "I don't know, of course. The thing is, to me, he seemed like someone out of control, but whether he'd want to kill someone... My instincts would say he was too shallow for that."

"No record of his going to the clinic or any emergency rooms," Torre said with a sigh of frustration. "So who would set his arm?"

"Are we talking about going to the police this time?" Jess asked with some disapproval in her voice.

"You want us to, Mom?" Maria asked.

"Not saying that, just wondered." Jess grinned. "Not to change the subject, but, of course, I am. Is anyone remembering that Lammas is almost here? Are we ever going to celebrate any of our festivals as a family?" This time her disapproval was clear.

"What does Lammas mean?" Nick asked. He looked over at Mitch. "I am not into this witchy stuff, in case you didn't know."

"You can learn," Elsa said with a flirtatious smile. She was something else. "This Sabbat is about the cycle of birth, life, death and rebirth, and in honor of Lugh, who is considered a warrior god of sorts but more than that. He was so much more than that. Even a bard." She turned that grin onto Mitch.

"As a skilled warrior, he had a magick spear. Some say when a lightning storm comes through, such as we had yesterday, it's Lugh fighting. Lugh is the god of the storms. And in that, I guess you both suit the mythology for Lughnasadh because you are both men of many skills—the warrior and the artist."

"And about that sacrificing part," Mitch quipped with a crooked smile. "What is there always about witches that leads to that somewhere?"

"This is more about gathering in and giving thanks for a good harvest," Jess said. "I am feeling particularly grateful this year for what my granddaughters have gathered in. Should we not celebrate that?"

"That's not totally true," Maria argued.

"What part?" Jess retorted.

"Well, Lugh is son of the Sun. The Sun God transfers his power into the grain, and is sacrificed when the grain is harvested. He will be reborn in the spring, of course, a resurrecting god, who dies for his people so they may live."

"Can we skip over the mythologies," Elke said, "and don't scare off this man by trying to say we are harvesting him." She laughed but didn't sound amused to Mitch.

"The question comes back to the police. Do we involve them this time?" Jess asked.

"There is something more," Elke said. "When I went out to the site they found the body, I tried to get a memory vision." She described it and ended with, "It was not Chuck Carter."

Mitch could see Maria mulling that over before she spoke. "Maybe two then. Could we be looking for two men, not one? And this idea of involving the police is difficult. Injuring a man, who was trying to break into Elke's apartment might not only cause him grief but give Elke publicity she does not need." She looked at Elke. "You had a strong feeling for the man was that night. I know it's not evidence in a court of law, but what was your instinct?"

"Pastor Jefferies. But when I talked to him, I asked if Chuck was in his church, and he acted as though he'd never heard of him."

"Was he lying?"

"I thought so. Debbie had worked for him," Elke said, "and he was upset with her wanting to be in plays and how she dressed. He found fault with my dress that day also."

"A pervert then," Elsa said. "They always talk the loudest about that sort of thing as a way to hide their own abuses."

"You go get the knife," Maria told Torre. "Make sure you protect it. I think we need to bring it here and see what we can get from it-- beyond the fingerprints." She looked then at Mitch. "Unless you disagree."

He smiled understanding that objects often stored memories. It wasn't his expertise to tap into that, but maybe witches could. "No problem to me however you go at it." He told Torre where it would be, if it had not already been found.

Celia came to the door. "When you folks are ready for lunch, it's ready for you."

Mitch found the abrupt change of mood to be a little surprising, but it worked for him, as they turned to small talk and eating while they waited for the knife. Nick sat beside him at the long table. "I read your book," Nick said.

"I have your painting—the one of a woman sitting on a boulder," Mitch responded.

"Ah yes, *Contemplation*. She looks a lot like Elke doesn't she?"

"In an impressionistic sort of way. How did you like the book?"

"To be honest, Denali wanted me to read it. I am not much into the mystical side of life—despite being married into this family and seeing things I hadn't expected. Your book though is good, lots of action, as though you knew of what you wrote."

"All fiction, of course," Mitch said.

"Of course." Nick chuckled. "Did you know Adolfo... or are you him?"

"Now, would you tell me who posed for your painting that I own?"

"All fictional, of course." They both laughed.

Mitch found the conversation that swirled around him to be amusing in a strange sort of way. His had been a world mostly of men. Around this table was a world of women, very different women from any he had known. It made him think about writing another book but with a female hero. Then he knew he shouldn't do that. One mistake was enough.

Torre returned with a plastic wrapped package and sat at the table to eat. "So you created Vislogus wine," she said with a smile.

"Jacques Durand more accurately, but I own the vineyard and winery. I'm his lackey is more accurate to how it works."

"Smart," Elsa said. "You recognize genius and protect it."

"I try."

"Does family get a discount?" Torre asked.

Elke swatted her. "You are a brat."

"Don't give her one," Denali said. "I tried to get a discount on the last dresses I needed, and they flat out turned me down. Family gets no discounts." She laughed.

When they returned to the living room, Torre, using plastic gloves, unwrapped the package and laid the knife on the table. Unsurprising to Mitch, since he was not into distant imaging, he got nothing from it. He saw the women concentrate, each in their own way with some closing their eyes and others staring at the blade. It wasn't particularly notable nor was the blade longer than eight inches. It wasn't intended as a weapon but as a tool so far as he could tell. He tried to use it to see the man again, but he got nothing. He did feel the energy in the room heighten.

Denali looked up and met his gaze. She said nothing as she sat back. Soon the women had all settled back. Maria stood. "We should go in a circle and share what we got. Starting with Denali because she is actually best at this."

"All right," Denali said, "but it's a bit chaotic. I did see the man coming to the gate, and Mitch do what he said, with a warning and brief struggle before the man ran away... I tried to go backward from that but couldn't get anything. What I did get was seeing where he went when he left. Faith in Action. A man came out of the church when he rang a bell. The man yelled at him but then let him into the church. I couldn't follow, but saw again when the man left with his arm in a sling."

"The pastor?" Elke asked.

"What does he look like?" Denali asked.

Torre pulled up a church image on her iPad. The pastor stood in front of his church.

"Yes, that's the man. I couldn't catch the words they exchanged, but the pastor was clearly furious and yet he must have helped him when inside."

"We need to do deeper research on Martin Jefferies and his history. It may have been the wrong direction with Charles Carter since that might be an assumed name with so little out there on him. Can I use your computer, Mom?" Torre asked. She headed for a room Mitch assumed must be a den. He felt a little shaken by what Denali had claimed. Much as he'd learned about the spirit world, he'd never done anything like that or even wanted to. He wondered how accurate it was.

"It has been before," Elke said putting her arm around his neck as she clearly read his body language if not his thoughts. "If she's right, then there is a connection with Chuck Carter and not only Debbie but the pastor. I could believe it given how deceptive I felt he was with me. Strange given his brother David is such a nice guy."

"And Bill or at least he's always been fair to me."

"What about the rest of you," Maria said. "What did the energy from the knife tell you?"

"I couldn't see anything," Elke said, "but I was probably too close to it."

"I felt that the one with the knife had come on an impulse," Jess said. "I could ask my guides."

Mitch thought of Nantan's unwillingness to help him and wondered how much good that would do.

Elsa cleared her throat. "I believe the man with the knife had had a recent tragedy. He was confused and trying to get himself together. He blamed himself at the same time he justified it was an accident."

"Accident?" Maria asked.

"I didn't get names."

"Did anyone find out what killed the girl?" Mitch asked, beginning to put together a story.

"I didn't ask Jace, but maybe I should," Maria said. "I'll be right back." She went into the other room to make a call.

"Anyone want a glass of wine?" Elke asked, looking around the room and then opening a bottle and giving those who had said yes a glass. Mitch was in no mood for alcohol. He needed a clear head.

When Maria returned, she said, "Jace said it was a head injury. Someone had hit her several times and then crushed her skull."

"So it could have been a beating and an accidental death?" Mitch asked.

"He didn't say that, but clearly it could have been if she was thrown down."

"That so strikes me as what Chuck Carter could have done," Elke said. "He just doesn't seem he has enough gumption for a murder. He is pathetic but not diabolical. Too stupid for that. But he wasn't the man I saw in the draw. Of course, maybe I was wrong."

"I don't think so," Elsa said. "The more I think on this, the more I see it as an accident but that had to be covered up. The question is why would that person help him?"

"If Carter was beating her and she fell, legally it would still be a degree of murder, whatever his intent," Mitch said.

"He's right," Nick agreed. "And it doesn't sound like he'd want to accept responsibility. I wonder where the death happened."

"I think an apartment," Devi spoke up for the first time. "I felt like he wanted to escape there after it happened."

"The thing is why would Jefferies help him if he's the one who took the body to the wash?"

Torre came out of the den. "The story is complicated. It turns out Jefferies had left Tucson and lived some years in Nebraska, had a family where Charles Carter was his stepson. They showed up here about six months apart. Chuck Carter was making virtually no money, had no job, yet he had a nice apartment. Most likely he was black-mailing Martin that he'd reveal that he had a family elsewhere. So far, I've seen no record of divorce. None of this can be proven as a motive for helping Carter, of course, but it would explain a lot."

"God, you are good at the computer," Mitch said feeling astounded.

"I pay for a detective site," Torre said with a grin. "You'd be amazed at what they have."

"I don't like how these murders end up looking unsolved," Nick said and rose to look out the window. Mitch understood his concern as a possible suspect. Sometimes that's all it took to nail someone or come looking at him anytime anything happened.

"What if we could connect it to Chuck this time," Elsa said with a little laugh. Mitch didn't see the humor in any of this.

"How?" Maria asked.

"It depends on where the accident happened. If it was Chuck's apartment, then there is physical evidence there. Even if it was where Debbie lived, fingerprints and blood might connect him. We need to find a reason for the police to get a warrant and search first Carter's apartment."

"And what would that take?" Elke asked.

"First, we put the knife back. Elke reports him physically accosting her. You did say he did that, right?"

Elke nodded.

"So, she reports that as well as her boyfriend interrupting a break-in."

"Can we connect any of it to Martin Jefferies?" Elke asked. Mitch understood that was her bigger concern as it would help their family.

"I don't see how," Torre said. "It seems obvious to me that Martin was not only trying to help his former stepson, but something more— create fear in the community. Unless Chuck wants to tie him into it, I don't think there will be evidence. Even the relationship might not come up-- unless one of the local reporters gets curious. The big thing is to get this murder settled, and I agree. I'll put the knife back where it was."

"It's been a week. How do we explain my waiting to report the attempted break-in?" Elke asked. Mitch liked how her mind worked. She thought like a writer.

"Trauma. Fear. And Mitch took you north to try to calm you down. You felt embarrassed and hated to admit what had happened twice before and nearly again," Maria suggested. "Jace will accept that." She grinned. "I am sure he will."

"And that will lead him to search Carter's apartment?" Nick asked.

"Of course, for more weapons, after he finds the knife, with fingerprints. It would create a pattern," Maria said sounding very confident. "Blood there will match the girl's, and he'll be on his way to prison even if it's only for manslaughter."

"It could work," Nick agreed. "It still leaves two unsolved murders, but they are further back, so…"

"And it lets Martin off the hook," Elke said, still sounding annoyed.

"His kind always gets his eventually," Jess said with that grandmotherly sound that Mitch had never heard in his personal life but liked. He was surprised how much he liked being with these women, listening to their thinking, their teasing, even their squabbling.

"I'd rather he got it sooner than later," Elke protested. "I have a feeling he is guilty of more than going after us."

"Trust me, granddaughter," Jess said, "it'll not work well for him. Why don't we take one of them at a time?"

Maria nodded her agreement.

"All right," Elke said, "I'll call the police when I get back to my apartment."

"Now," Jess said, "tell us about what happened up north with the Rugaru." Her smirk increased when she saw Elsa didn't know what she was talking about.

"A swamp monster?" Elsa asked.

"Native American too," Jess retorted.

So Mitch sat back and let Elke tell the story of their encounter with the monster.

"I always thought they were real," Denali said. "People should have more faith in the basis for mythologies."

"You did kill it though, and it was the same as in your book?" Maria asked.

"It seems they breed and who knows how many in various places —serving demons maybe?" Mitch asked. "They seem to favor water though, so strange if it'd be in the desert."

"You said your cousin was suckered in," Torre suggested.

"Yes, and apologetic," Mitch said.

"Well, it will be good we start getting more alert. We have gotten lax," Jess said. "All the more reason to celebrate Lammas and not forget our important rituals and events." When no one argued with her, including Elsa, she smiled with satisfaction.

When Mitch and Elke were back on the street, she said, "Are you heading north now?"

"Why would you ask that?" He tried to follow her logic but found it impossible.

"Well, you won't want the publicity this could bring on you. I know you avoid that. I can keep your name out of it..."

He stopped her, swung her into his arms. It was too hot for that, but he didn't care. He laughed. "Listen to me, baby, and get it straight. It's too late for me to avoid the problems you will bring my life." She gave a little snort. "Will you marry me?"

"What?"

"You heard me."

"You mean it?" She sounded shocked.

"I do. When we get this straightened out, and we will, then yes, I want to go north, but with you as my wife. Did you want a big wedding? Or wait, you haven't said yes yet."

She smiled then. "Yes, I'd like to be your wife."

"Good. So let's head back to your apartment to celebrate, then you can call your mama and grandmas and tell them to plan something small so we can be north for the grape harvest. If Carter slows us down, I'll take care of him myself."

"I believe you mean that."

"You can bet on it. Now let's get this whole thing started as I am anxious for the next scene."

"We have to wait for that?" she asked pulling his head down for a searing kiss.

Probably not.

EPILOGUE

"You thought you were so clever, didn't you?" Azaziel snarled.

"I thought it would go well," Ornis replied, trying for a placating tone when he didn't feel it. He never felt it.

"Ah yes, so well." The sneer turned what was a cruel face even darker.

The two watched as the party of horsemen rode out of the ranch yard, heading for what the two demons knew was their sacred ground-- where they'd not be able to follow or know what they did. Being it was Lammas, it was obvious they would be doing a harvest celebration. Boring in Ornis' mind. Why were they even watching them ride?

"The only blessing... if I may use the word loosely," Azaziel said with an unpleasant cackle, "is at least you didn't cost us our pastor. He will continue with the demonstrations, and if we get fortunate, we'll find someone in his congregation open to using more violent means to right wrongs. As a bonus, he for now can quit worrying about that stupid stepson of his."

"Not actually a stepson since his marriage to the lad's mother was never a real one," Ornis said, then ducked back to avoid Azaziel's swipe of his fist. Being of the spirit, it wasn't actually a fist, but it would have been painful in terms of demeaning. Maybe it would have eased the anger of his superior. He should have let him hit him.

"Just as well he's in jail. He was a pathetic distraction."

"Then all is well," Ornis said as he thought—that wasn't what you believed before.

Azaziel snarled, as they watched two powerful men nudge their horses in the side and take off at a hard run. "You think that is well." He snorted. "Before, we had all women to deal with, and yes, they are powerful witches but still… they weren't as engaged as they might have been. Now, two men, both warriors, one a powerful wizard on his own right, have come into their fold. Soon Ford will be married and even more engaged in the problems of the Hemstreets."

"I didn't intend that to happen."

Another snort of derision. "Intentions don't count. Only results. You have toyed with insignificant battles, diversions, and now you see in place something far more dangerous for our goals. Do you understand that?" Azaziel gave him a hostile look.

"Are you removing me from the Tucson district?" Ornis asked thinking that might not be so bad. He wouldn't mind a change of scene. He liked Wyoming with less people and more open spaces. He could…

"No," Azaziel interrupted his pleasant train of thought, "I am making it clear that the consequences of losing again will be catastrophic for you. It won't just result in a demotion." He made an imaginary slice across his throat.

Ornis nodded. "I understand." He actually didn't as he felt he'd been pretty effective in strewing chaos. Unfortunately, at least for now, it wasn't his opinion that counted.

"You used to be good at manipulating people, but you seem to have lost that ability."

"It was not my responsibility in the Verde. That was John Scythe's job. He used the wrong tool with Joe."

"Tools, you mean."

"All right tools. Although I rather liked the Rugarus. Such a shame how those two ended up."

"It has some advantages as there are those in their pack, who want revenge."

"You mean against Ford?"

"Among others. They will wait for their chance."

Ornis tried to think through exactly what was being suggested. "You want one of them to come to Tucson? I thought they mostly stayed in the wilderness."

"They go where they are told, but I meant in this case, we need a human to use."

Ornis tried to work through what that meant. "The pastor?"

"You are so stupid. There is a weak link among the sisters."

Ornis tried to think whom he might mean. "Devi?" he asked finally thinking of the shy sister. She did appear weak.

"You are not totally stupid. Yes, her. She does not want to be a witch. She dabbles in potions and plants, but she doubts. She can be used."

"How would that work out?" He felt clueless and hated the feeling.

"She would let us put someone into their family, someone who will weaken the links."

"A man?"

"You truly are stupid. Of course, a man. One who is trying to gain power for himself using other humans."

"This person is not into magick?" It would be easier to manipulate him if he was.

"He doesn't believe in it, but he wants power. He has an energy in him that he doesn't yet recognize. We would not need to manage him. He would do it all on his own."

"Why would she want someone like that? She seems like a very nice person and that does not sound like a nice man."

"Because she's young and naïve. Because he is strong where she is not."

"So we won't try to manipulate him?"

"No need." Azaziel chuckled. "Some humans do it for us. His strength will be his weakness. It will draw her to him."

"I don't see why he'd want her then. Is he cruel and needs someone weak?"

"No, he needs a puppet, someone who won't get in his way. That's her."

∾

None of this sounded logical to Ornis. He liked the idea though that this plan was on Azaziel's shoulders—whichever way it went down. He could go for that. Maybe even see Azaziel taken down a notch when the Hemstreet witches saw what was happening. He smirked. This was a win/win. "So what is my part in it?"

If you enjoyed this book, please leave a review where you bought it. Even a few words mean a lot to future potential readers as well as writers. A review is your opportunity to be part of the creative process.

For any questions, contact Rain
raintrueax@gmail.com

Follow the Hemstreet Witches Series with Book 3.
'Little Devi' isn't quite as weak as the demons imagine, and their judgment of the man is based on the past, not who he is today. Demons don't know it all and particularly easily misjudge ones they hope to use.

Denali and Nick's story, Book 1, *Enchantress' Secret*:

More about Rain and her other books, contemporary, historical, and paranormal at:

http://www.facebook.com/RainTrueax/

http://rainydaythought.blogspot.com/

http://romanceswithanedge.blogspot.com